No Just Desserts

No Just Desserts

Elisabeth Bastion

Five Star • Waterville, Maine

Published in 2005 in conjunction with Tekno Books and Ed Gorman.

Set in 11 pt. Plantin.

Printed in the United States on permanent paper.

Library of Congress Cataloging-in-Publication Data

Bastion, Elisabeth.
    No just desserts / Elisabeth Bastion.
      p. cm.
    ISBN 1-59414-192-4 (hc : alk. paper)
    ISBN 1-4104-0239-8 (sc : alk. paper)
     1. Women public relations personnel—Fiction.
2. Cookery—Competitions—Fiction. 3. Americans—England—Fiction. 4. London (England)—Fiction.
5. Cookery—Fiction. 6. Cooks—Fiction. I. Title.
    PS3602.A8495N6 2004
    813'.6—dc22   2004043305

To my husband, Michael Varese,
and to the long-suffering listeners at
Marijane Meaker's Ashawagh Hall
Writers' Workshop.

Chapter 1

Don't try to convince me that the British are shining examples of fair play, good sportsmanship and splendid manners. I have been working here in the London office of my big ad agency for less than one week, and already I've been hit by food poisoning given me by their very own test kitchen. Then I received a really nasty note through the interoffice mail, an actual threatening letter. Now, I know Americans are not popular in most parts of the world, but this is going too far. Way, way too far.

"So frightfully sorry, Lucille," the head of the test kitchen said later in apology, "but it's never happened before. A freak accident."

I'll go along with that. But I have that note right here in my handbag—the note that came through the office mail, looking oh so innocent in its little buff envelope. This is no freak accident. This is deliberate malice.

It wasn't my idea to get this temporary assignment in the London office of MWVB. I couldn't have been more surprised when my boss, Barry Boyle, called me into his office that fateful day in New York City and asked if I could see my way clear to spending time in London, helping that office to launch a product called "Sweet Whippo." He went on and on about what a great job I had just done with the public relations part of the national launch of a new food product. Apparently branches around the world had read about it in the company newsletter and now London Office had made an official request for me to give them my valuable advice and help by working there for six weeks.

"What is this product 'Sweet Whippo' anyhow," I asked. "Sounds disgusting. Even violent. Whippo!"

"I'm not really sure, Lucille," Barry admitted. "I'm told it is one of these new synthetic compounds, but not a prescription product. It has no fat, no cholesterol, no sugar, no salt, practically no calories, yet it is full of fiber. It replaces all the evil things in many products and is even supposed to improve flavor. It seems that it has already been added to some manufactured specialty foods over there, but now its maker wants to show the home cook how to use it."

"I've never heard of it," I said.

"Neither have I, but I was told companies around the world are fast developing similar products, competing like hell, and London Office wants to be the first with this big launch for their client. We don't have the stuff over here, I'm told."

"I hope not."

Barry ignored my comment. "London Office needs your brains," he went on. "Apparently they've had some doubts about their current approach." His grin was wolfish. I knew there was no love lost between him and the head of the public relations department in London.

"I thought London never wanted any advice from the New York Office. Especially from our little PR group."

Barry nodded. "John Bowen had no choice. The new World Chairman suggested it. He wants the campaign to be both British and American in approach—mid-Atlantic, hands across the sea, all that stuff."

"Sounds impossible to me."

"Oh, come on, Lucille, you can handle this assignment. You're always saying London is your favorite city in the world, and here you have a chance to go there first class for six weeks. They need a senior executive like you to show them how we do things so well."

I tried not to wince at the words "senior executive." True, I'm now considered one of the old timers because I've been here for ten years. We've had a slew of bright, young PR types come and go, especially when they learned that there was no glamour involved and too much hard work. Bitterly disappointed, some of them were, and went off looking for better shops with more celebrity work. I certainly encouraged their departure and happily stayed on. But mid-forties means I'm in my prime, no gray hair, all my own teeth. In fact, I've never looked better, really good for my age. My weight is almost down to the right level, thanks to Weight Watchers and Pilates classes, and my clothes really show off my reworked body. My new hair color—streaky, dark blonde—makes my brown eyes look brighter. Forget "senior."

Barry went on. "Six weeks at most, big expense account, and listen, Lucille, think of it as a big plus for you, a way to help me convince management you're worth the big bucks I pay you. It's a rough time now, as you know, and a lot of people, cheaper people, want your job. This new worldwide guy is breathing down my neck."

I wished he hadn't said that. No job is secure these days but I had thought I was safe. Who was after my job? Would Barry tell me?

Actually, the assignment sounded wonderful. I could do with an expense-account stay in London. I really deserved some time there after my recent treks to North Dakota, Nebraska, Mississippi and Arkansas, where I'd had to show up on local television, courting the local food editors, doing demonstrations at the gas companies showing their audiences the incredible joys of using a new product called "Goodsauce." Even guest shots on the Food Channel don't count like real personal appearances.

As much as I didn't want to admit it, even to myself, this trip might also help to clear up the standoff I've been in with Danny. We've been together too long without making it legal, he says, but I am still undecided. "You'll stay in the company's apartment in London, a truly elegant one, I'm told," Barry purred, piling it on. "Nice people in their Public Relations Department. Think of how you can use that experience when you come back here, especially as Senior Vice President."

That word "senior" again. But I can bargain, too. "If I do this assignment, promise me I won't have to do any more food publicity for these awful food products, especially the ones made out of synthetics which are probably killing us all. Promise me I can work on something real, some natural food, something actually good for you. Nothing genetically modified. Better still, take me off these campaigns. I am beginning to feel guilty about foisting food ideas on my fellow consumers. I know, I know," I added quickly, as I saw Barry frown, "I liked working in food at first and I enjoyed all those cooking courses I took and the wonderful restaurants I got to eat in, but things are getting out of hand. I'm basically a writer, not a trained chef."

"I won't take you off the work because you are too good and it's too lucrative for the agency. But I will consider putting you on some new accounts, the ones you call 'real food.' We're pitching for two big ones now, and if we're lucky, you'll have a chance to be in charge."

Of course I took the assignment. But in just these few

days it's been trouble from start to finish, capped by that disgusting note. What happened to all those nice people in London Office?

Chapter 2

The first few days in London were good; in fact, downright marvelous, especially after all the rushing around I had to do to put my New York life on hold. Danny hadn't been thrilled about this absence or to be put in charge of looking after our plants and forwarding mail. Things had been tense between us lately. He wanted a commitment, but I wasn't sure I did. Not with him, anyhow. I like my freedom and part of me still hasn't grown up. It's the part that wants to write mysteries; in fact, the part that wants to live those mysteries.

You see, I have this guilty secret. I am an addict, a mystery story addict of the worst kind because I am obsessed with English mysteries. I have read all the classic British writers—Agatha Christie, Dorothy Sayers, Ngaio Marsh, Daphne du Maurier, and I now pounce upon anything by P. D. James, Ruth Rendell and Colin Dexter and anyone else who tells me a tale of wrongdoings among Cotswold cottages or Dorset manor houses. I am glued to my television set every time there's a mystery with Inspector Morse, Hercule Poirot, or Frost. "Masterpiece Theater," even the reruns, is my cocaine. I confess that I also have the videos of all my favorites, which I watch, ruled pad in hand, making notes. This drives Danny crazy. I love plots set in London, too, providing they are in Kensington, Chelsea,

Marylebone or Mayfair—none of the seamier suburbs for me. I don't enjoy mysteries with blood, guts, terrorists, fiery explosions or those which have heroes with designer stubble faces. I don't need to read sweaty, grunty, heavy-breathing sex scenes. I consider them best for male wannabes. Maybe I am a Miss Marple at heart, but with a good sex life. I have yet another confession. I am writing a mystery myself, part of it to be set in England. How's that for fortuitous timing? Now I have this unexpected chance to get first-hand knowledge. I can see it all now: Lucille Anderson, clever amateur American detective, helping Scotland Yard solve a complicated crime. Dream on, Lucille.

Back to Sweet Whippo and the people who pay my salary.

I couldn't talk Barry into letting me spend his budget on flying first class, but at least I didn't have to take the overnight red-eye. I arrived in London on a late Sunday evening in the last week of May, Business Class all the way. As promised, I was met at Heathrow by Will Hammersmith, one of London Office's top people, and Fiona Gordon, head of the Test Kitchen. Will was every inch the handsome, fair-haired, blue-eyed Englishman, well turned out in a beautifully cut blazer, blue shirt, ascot and chinos. Informal wear for Sunday night airport trips. The Hugh Grant type. Fiona, a striking, glossy black-haired, tall woman, was more formally dressed in a green-patterned silk dress with a short black jacket and shiny black shoes with very high heels. A Diana Rigg look-alike. When they looked *me* over, I was immediately aware that I brought down the tone of this meeting with my travel-rumpled black slacks and jacket, and the low-heeled shoes I considered necessary for those long hikes through Heathrow. Wait until I show up for work

13

in London Office in my newest Donna Karan dark red suit and an ivory silk blouse, an outfit which makes me look tall and thin and incredibly successful.

These two paragons escorted me to the company flat via Will's big black Jaguar. On the trip in, he was charming, efficient and chatty, but Fiona was cool and distant. Did this mean there would be trouble ahead with her and her kitchen? I had to work closely with her for recipe development if we were going to make the combined-countries approach work. Perhaps cool and distant was just her manner.

The drive was fast and smooth through the London suburbs, and it was exciting to see London again on this clear, just-getting-dark evening. These long, long twilights in May and June are hard to beat. A final swing through Hyde Park and past Grosvenor Square took us to a tall, dark-stone apartment building. Will pulled up in front of it, helped me organize my luggage and one duty-free bag (I had restrained my shopping on the plane) for the porter to take up, left the car parked and led us into the elevator.

Will opened the door to the flat and ceremoniously handed me the key. Fiona pushed by him and asked, "Mind if I look round the flat? This is a new one and I haven't seen it. It does look posh. I'd like to check out the kitchen."

While she was wandering through the rooms, Will gave me directions to the office, which was only four blocks away, and mentioned that the flat had a "daily," a cleaning woman who came in every morning for a couple of hours. Now *that* is luxury. I walked over to the window. The flat was on the tenth floor and I could see Hyde Park, its green pastures and tall trees. I turned and surveyed the living room. It was furnished in antique furniture—or good reproductions, probably Regency, because I can't tell the difference. The tall windows hung with dark rose and blue curtains picked up the colors of the large oriental rug.

"Don't try to come into the office tomorrow," Will said. "You'll need a couple of days to get settled and get over jet lag. I'll be away and the Whippo client is on the Continent. Come in on, say, Wednesday."

I started to ask him questions about the account, ever the eager PR executive, but he shrugged them off. "You'll soon see," he promised. It sounded ominous.

Fiona came back into the room carrying a bottle of champagne. "Look what I found in the fridge. What do you say we have a glass of bubbly to celebrate the new mid-Atlantic alliance? There are glasses on the drinks trolley behind you, Will."

He frowned but held out his hand for the bottle, opened it with a minimum of splashing and poured the drinks. The last thing I needed was champagne after the drinks and wine on the plane, but I felt it polite to sip away. I couldn't quite figure out the relationship between these two. Fiona was definitely making this into a social occasion, but whether it was for my benefit or for Will's, I couldn't tell. On the way in she had mentioned their wonderful dinner together. They took their time, sipping away, chatting, gave me a real once-over in a subtle British way with no direct looks, just those old Princess Di sidelong glances.

"We *were* a bit surprised to hear you were coming over," Will admitted, "but John Bowen was following orders from our World Chairman, of course, and Fiona and I will see that you find enough to do."

He made it plain that it wasn't their idea for me to be here, and I didn't like that expression "find enough to do." I could see myself sitting in a corner leafing through British food magazines. Finally, after the bottle—my bottle—was finished, they departed, Fiona with her arm through Will's.

I didn't exactly feel overwhelmed by the warmth of their welcome.

I used those precious two days to immerse myself in the local scene. London had changed in the last three years. I became very aware—was it my age?—that the people on the street looked much younger, except for a surprising number of older, rougher, poorly dressed men and women. On my last trip, I had been used to seeing Indians, Pakistanis, Caribbeans, Arabs and Asians, along with the usual Anglo-Saxon faces, blondes and redheads, crowding the streets. But this new group puzzled me.

"Refugees, thousands of them," the doorman told me when I asked. "Getting here any way they can from Europe, in small boats across the Channel, even stowing away by riding under the Eurostar. From Bosnia, Serbia, Russia, North Africa, even Afghanistan. Calling themselves 'Asylum Seekers.' Causing welfare problems. Crime, too." His face was so stony that I didn't pursue the subject.

There was the usual assortment of men, women and children walking around with mobile telephones glued to their ears and there were long lines at ATM machines. And there seemed to be millions of teenage tourists, all jabbering in languages I couldn't recognize. London looked more like New York City than it had when I was last here. Even more crowded, if possible.

The country also seemed to have gone crazy over food. I'd read about the food revolution that had taken place, maybe because of the European Common Market influence. England's well-known fondness for solid, overcooked food seemed to have been replaced by a new cuisine of both exotic and gourmet treatment of basic food. On the television, I saw more programs featuring food in two days and

nights than I'd seen in weeks back home, even with the new
and glamorous Brits Nigella and the super competent Delia
on PBS. These programs were in prime time on the BBC
and the commercial channels. There were chefs, food
writers, film and stage celebrities, men, women and even
children, all demonstrating, preparing, talking, judging and
stuffing every kind of food into their mouths in front of millions of viewers. There were food quizzes with big prizes
and cooking contests done against the clock. There were
more food programs on cable, too—some imported from
America—but after a while I ran out of time and eyeballs. I
wondered why London Office needed more food ideas after
this glut of information.

My biggest problem was that measures were in metric,
still alien to me. Ever try to figure out how many potatoes
in a kilo? I had a handy conversion table I'd brought over,
and no one seemed to notice me standing in the supermarket aisle working quantities out. And the prices!
London food prices were the highest I'd ever seen, even
more than Paris, I was told.

I checked out the supermarkets and the grocery sections
of all the big department stores. As I stood staring at the
counters in my local supermarket holding fish I had never
seen before, I thought, Lucille, how can you even think
about introducing yet another product to the British con-
sumer—and a totally synthetic and probably ugly one, at
that? Why did you take on this assignment? Why did you let
Barry talk you into this? There's still time to back out before London Office finds out how provincial you really are.

I was tempted, but I gritted my teeth and read up on
cooking in all the glossy food magazines, trying some of
their recipes on the flat's unfamiliar stove. Translating Cel-
sius into Fahrenheit still threw me, and so I overcooked or

undercooked some recipes in my oven. I did get help from my "daily," Mrs. Lucas, who showed up each morning to police the flat. She helped me prepare some of the vegetables and fruits I had lugged home and translated what the instructions said on the packages. I liked all the little signs on the labels: Suitable for Home Freezing, Product of Spain (or Turkey or France or South Africa, even U.S.), Suitable for Vegetarians, Not Suitable for Persons with Nut Allergies, Ready to Cook—plus all the ingredients, calorie count (called Energy), etc., etc. All this was in at least three languages, too. We had a few good laughs at my ignorance and the battle with the cooker, as she called the stove.

I despaired of my culinary future here.

Everyone was welcoming on my first day at the office, all smiles and jollity, with introductions all around by Will. He explained to us that even though ordinarily he did not concern himself too much with the public relations side, he would personally be involved in this launch.

"So much at stake, you know, with such a new and controversial product."

My heart sank. "Controversial?" Nobody had told me "controversial."

I was given the visiting VIP treatment, complete with a small, private office adjoining the cubicle of the public relations executive on this account. Her name was Jane Mallow and I liked her right away. Dressed in black pants, loose green top and ankle boots, she was slightly plump with an open, freckled face, a head of gorgeous red hair and a welcoming smile. I guessed her to be in her late twenties. She was friendly and funny as she filled me in on what had been done so far on Sweet Whippo.

"I must tell you that this is the very first food account

that I've been assigned to," she added. "Just been promoted from Junior Publicist, you know. I'm ever so excited!"

My heart sank again as I realized I would be working with someone still learning about food publicity. I had hoped for an old timer to fill *me* in on the British food campaigns. But Jane would obviously do her eager best. She gave me a stack of plans and programs for Sweet Whippo which I took back to my office, piled on my desk with its absolutely empty and spotless top, and started in reading. Back she bounced again with a few proposed recipes for the product, all done in the baffling kilos and milligrams. I felt lost.

Then came disaster.

Summoned later that morning to a tasting of the initial recipes previously produced for Sweet Whippo, I dutifully went down with Jane to the test kitchens located in the basement of the building. Here were two rooms full of stoves, refrigerators, freezers, microwaves, food processors, dishwashers and a few appliances I couldn't recognize. Fiona welcomed me and introduced her staff—three young women attired in black slacks with covering aprons or smocks. One girl was Japanese, a second was Indian, and a third was introduced as her second in command, Pauline Greene, from Dorset. Ethnically, Fiona certainly had her food bases covered. She herself did not look like the usual home economist back home. She had on a white lab coat over a dark red silky dress and she tripped around in yet another pair of high-heeled shoes, these dark red. How she could work in those things? Fiona's shiny black hair was apparently never ever subjected to any hair net and she tossed it around freely as she spoke. No sanitation qualms here. Pauline, on the other hand, was her opposite—a stocky woman with straw-colored straight hair pulled back and held firmly with barrettes and attired in a dark blue smock worn over denims. Her feet were shod in sensible dark brown walking shoes. So far I'd noticed that London Office dress code included everything from semi-formal to dressed-down types.

There were three desserts laid out on a tray, and I was asked to eat a few spoonfuls from each and give them my comments.

"We did these yesterday and we were very pleased," Pauline said, handing me the first spoon. "I think you'll agree. We want an American opinion," she explained to Jane, bypassing her. Jane eyed the plates but didn't comment.

I tasted the first offering, chewing away slowly while five pairs of eyes solemnly watched me. This specialty was a meringue filled with unidentifiable purple glop, labeled Meringue Black-currant Frappe. I nodded wisely, went "mmmm," took a drink from the glass of water offered and accepted the clean fork handed me. I took a helping of a small greenish cake called Pistachio Crème Gateau, masticated it thoroughly, then had another sip of water. You'd have thought I was tasting caviar the way Fiona's staff beamed. The last spoonful I took was labeled Whipped Gooseberry Jelly. It was a dish of wobbly pink gelatin with sliced gooseberries. It was so sour that I felt like spitting it out, but instead swallowed dutifully, forcing myself not to make a face. Gooseberries here must be very tart indeed.

I didn't really thrill to any of the desserts, but I said they were certainly interesting and new tastes for my American palate. Fiona and Pauline looked disappointed, but I swear that Caro, the Japanese woman, gave me a sympathetic smile.

Then we all sat down and looked at the giant container

of Sweet Whippo, which had been reverently taken from the refrigerator. It was opened and the contents shown to me. I stared with dismay at the quivering, oyster-colored liquid. Talk about revolting. This was going to be worse than my problems back in the states with Goodsauce, and God knows that was just a simple synthetic sweetener product, not this stuff which was touted to be the first of its kind ever produced on the entire globe and could solve the diet problems of the British Isles.

I wanted to ask about "controversial," but Fiona and Pauline were obviously thrilled and enthusiastic about the first recipe development with Sweet Whippo. They now eagerly awaited my contribution of good American ideas for use of the product. Or so they said.

I gave them a few ideas off the top of my head (some of them left over from our introduction of Goodsauce in the U.S.), but they didn't seem to thrill to the idea of Pumpkin Chiffon Pie or Blueberry Shortcake. When I mentioned going into main dishes and vegetables, such as Meatloaf with Spicy Sauce or Eggplant with Cheese Topping, Pauline made a face and Fiona actually snorted.

"We call it aubergine, your eggplant, I mean," she said in a patronizing voice.

"Whatever," I countered. "It's a good vegetable for a sauce made with Sweet Whippo."

I went on with a few more ideas, such as Barbecued Ribs or Turkey à la King. Jane was silent, but nodded her head encouragingly.

"I'd like the kitchen to work on these ideas," I said, handing over the sheet of paper with more suggestions for dishes using that gloppy product. I was trying to come across as the high-powered food expert. "I'll work with you to turn them into finished recipes."

Fiona took the proffered paper, read a few lines, shrugged and handed it to Pauline. There was an eloquent silence as Pauline pored over it. I looked over at Jane, but she kept her face diplomatically neutral. All of a sudden, I got a sharp quick pain in my stomach. I asked for a glass of water. Caro handed it to me, concern on her face. I must have looked sick, and truthfully I was beginning to feel queasy. I am known for my cast iron stomach (I need it, working in food publicity), but those sickly sweet desserts had definitely stirred it up. The silence lingered as Pauline kept reading, obvious disbelief on her face.

My stomach gave me another sharp pain and I suddenly felt hot. Sweat broke out on my forehead, and I knew I needed to get out of there. As I stood up to depart, my stomach suddenly rebelled. It started churning away and I knew I was about to lose those Sweet Whippo delights.

"Quick, Fiona, the bathroom?" I asked and followed her pointing finger to a door close by. It opened into a small bathroom and I got inside just in time. I knew that Jane, Fiona and all her staff could hear the unmistakable sounds of me throwing up. Those damn sweet desserts were poisonous all right. But why was I having such a violent reaction? My head started pounding and I felt sweaty all over. Dizziness forced me to sit on the cold floor. Could I possibly be dying with salmonella, maybe botulism? God, imagine breathing your last in the bathroom in a test kitchen, a London one at that. Should I yell for help, for an ambulance? Maybe it was a heart attack—after all I was over forty. No, I must not panic. Slowly, very slowly, the dizziness went away, my stomach quieted and my heart's pounding calmed. Pull yourself together, Lucille, I commanded, and after a tremendous effort of deep yoga breathing, I finally did. I had survived.

Chapter 3

Fiona was all concern and sympathy when I finally trailed back into the test kitchen, wiping my sweaty face with a tissue. I was both embarrassed and angry.

"What was in that last little glop of stuff you fed me? I thought it tasted far too sour, but I figured that was the way it was supposed to be. Did anyone else try it today?"

Puzzled and slightly amused looks passed among Fiona and her staff. They all shook their heads. Jane looked at me anxiously.

Fiona smiled sweetly at me. "Lucille, I am indeed chagrined at your violent reaction to our sweets, particularly that gooseberry jelly one. Perhaps you are allergic to gooseberries?"

"I never have been," I said. "We do have them in American you know. But I *am* worried that I might be allergic to Sweet Whippo, and if am, think of all the consumers in this country who also might be. I think I'd better talk to the manufacturer right away."

There were gasps from her staff and Fiona's face turned stony. Jane moaned gently and rolled her eyes at me. The look Fiona gave me was murderous and I knew from then on it was going to be a no-holds-barred contest between us. I didn't care because I could remember only too well how wretched my stomach felt.

"The client, the man in charge of the production of Whippo, is on the Continent this week, but as soon as he gets back, I'll talk to him," Fiona said.

"*We'll* talk to him," I said firmly. "And Jane, too."

We stared at each other, while her girls sat motionless, still as statues. Jane took a deep breath and held it. I stood up, beckoned Jane and together we walked out of the test kitchen. Jane turned to say something to Fiona, but I grabbed her arm firmly and we kept on walking. As soon as we got into the lift and out of earshot, she spoke.

"What are we going to do now?" she asked. "Fiona was furious."

"So was I. So am I. She tried to poison me with that stuff. I noticed she didn't ask you or any of her staff to taste it, even after I pointed it out as a killer."

Jane started to say more, but I ignored her and went on.

"Fiona and her merry maids obviously don't feel the need to cooperate," I said to her, "but they are going to have to do my bidding, or there'll be hell to pay."

We got out of the lift at our floor and Jane scurried back into her office while I stomped into mine, stomach still queasy and head beginning to ache. At my desk I put my head into my hands, but raised it quickly when Jane reappeared with a cup of tea—the British answer to all crises. She left quickly before I could start talking again.

I sat at my desk, sipping the tea, and thinking hard. I was determined to show this London Office that we Americans were made of stern stuff, but my stomach gave a lurch just then and I swallowed quickly. I put down the tea and started reading through the piles of paper on my desk, looking for any reports of adverse reaction to the slimy stuff.

Jane put her head around the door and asked if I wanted

an official welcoming lunch at a nice restaurant or perhaps, because of my stomach upset, just a sandwich at the pub across the street? The telephone rang just then and it turned out to be Fiona. She was all charm and light laughs and told me that one of her girls had just confessed that she had left that particular gooseberry jelly out of the fridge overnight, by mistake, she was most dreadfully sorry, hadn't realized that it would spoil; strange that I hadn't realized that it had gone off; it was just a freak accident, of course. And wasn't it wonderful that it wasn't a possible allergic reaction after all?

"Wonderful, Fiona, but that brings up yet one more problem. Maybe dishes made with Sweet Whippo can never stay out of a refrigerator for very long. Now we damn sure better talk to the client about the problems of dishes made with Sweet Whippo spoiling unless heavily refrigerated. How do we know it's not poisonous, even potentially lethal? I may have been just lucky that I only had a spoonful of that damn gooseberry dessert."

I could picture Fiona snarling at the other end of this telephone, but we talked on, coolly and a little more politely, both finally agreeing that we would certainly approach the client with these problems as soon as he got back from "Continent." That word again.

Jane seemed relieved to hear the story, but disappointed that I turned down the offer of the official welcoming lunch at the Connaught. I knew my stomach could not do justice to it, and instead went with her and two young men—colleagues from the Public Relations section—to the nearby Red Lion pub. Jane and these two men were nice, friendly types, full of questions about life in the New York Office, which apparently all of them wanted to hear about and be transferred to. I settled for a cheese sandwich and a glass of white wine. Nobody mentioned gooseberry jelly and my foray into the bathroom of the test kitchen, although I suspected that the news had flown throughout the agency with great speed.

After lunch I went back to my office and read more facts and figures on the dreaded product. After another hour, when I thought I had made my point about New York Office stamina, I put my head into Jane's office.

"At least I survived my first day here, Jane, but it wasn't easy. I'm going home."

She was on the telephone, but gave me a weak smile and a farewell wave.

The sun was shining, the air was cool and the walk back to the company flat led through Grosvenor Square and by a row of elegant shops. I stopped to look into one of them—no way I could afford that dress—and turned around to see a figure dash quickly around the corner. I stood for a minute thinking New York City thoughts—anyone running could mean a mugging or a purse snatching—but no one else on the street seemed perturbed.

You're in London now, Lucille, and there is less crime here, or so they say. It was probably a jogger and you're getting paranoid after that taste testing fiasco. I did look behind me several times for the last few blocks and I swear I saw a figure—I couldn't tell whether it was male or female—that seemed to stop when I stopped to look in a shop window and would start walking again when I did. I darted into a doorway—Miss Marple would certainly have approved—and waited. And waited. And waited some more. Schoolgirls went by, mothers with children went by, and two old men slowly walked by, talking quietly. One of the Asylum Seeker types also went by, who even stopped and looked hard at me before going on. I stepped out of my shelter defiantly and walked quickly to the flat. I think that gooseberry dish had started my ever-imaginative brain working overtime on possible disaster and death awaiting me in London. Was I starting in on my woman detective routine far too soon? Did I suspect those poor refugees were terrorists? Was 9/11 still too much on my mind? Why me? I wished I was back home.

In the flat, I made myself a gin and tonic, took a couple of Pepto-Bismols and sat down to think about the day, trying to forget my fears. Somehow, my disgrace in the test kitchen now had its funny side. I could hardly wait to tell Barry Boyle tomorrow and we could laugh together. We had always joked about test kitchens waiting to poison us and that lethal Whipped Gooseberry Jelly had almost made it. I made myself a big salad and opened a can of Baxter's Cream of Leek soup, watched television and went to bed. Danny called just before I dozed off and we had a good talk. I didn't tell him about the test kitchen disaster; I don't know why. After we talked, I felt much better about my time in London and decided that tomorrow I would be the cheery, smiling, perfect American and would show the entire office how well I could work with Fiona and Will and other assorted London Office people. All would go well now, I told myself, as I drifted off to sleep.

Then I walked into my office the next day and saw, sitting in the exact center of my desktop, a small buff envelope. I opened it, unfolded the paper inside and stood there reading the words on it. It took a while to sink in. There were just two lines, boldly printed with a felt tip pen.

"Bugger off now before something *really* nasty happens!"

Chapter 4

I looked at the note again, just to make sure I wasn't hallucinating. The buff-colored envelope was marked "Personal" and had my name neatly typed on it. When I first picked it up I figured that it was just another official form to deal with, as I had been signing several thousand of them ever since I got here, promising that I wouldn't be a burden on the National Health, National Debt, UK Social Security, was just a temporary visitor, not even paid in British pounds, and still drawing my salary in New York City, etc., etc.

Now, I've worked in public relations for many years and I've had my share of unpleasant memos from bosses, clients, fellow-workers, not to mention downright abusive ones about my expense account from our Accounting Department, but I have never been sent words such as these. "Bugger off before something *really* nasty happens." There are weirdos everywhere, Lucille, even here in this highly-respectable, classy, conservative and world-famous agency and now one has got hold of you. Remember yesterday when you thought you were being followed. Could it be a stalker?

In an effort to stay calm, I took a deep breath and focused my eyes on the walls of my temporary office. The ornately framed bucolic scenes were precisely hung, the light from the long French windows opposite reflected dully on their surfaces. My eyes then went to the paisley pattern on the upholstered twin chairs set neatly in front of my desk. The fabric was pristine as ever and the carpet at my feet stretching right to the door was dark blue and beautifully clean.

Yet something nasty had crept into my office, into my life. First the spoiled food, then someone possibly stalking me, and now this. Lucille, you wanted to learn about English crime at first hand, and this may be your first real lesson. Stop trembling and force yourself to calm down and think it through.

I took a deep breath, folded and replaced the note in its envelope and stuffed it into my handbag, snapping shut the clasp of the bag and replacing it in the bottom drawer of my desk, the one with the lock. I turned the key in it and stuck the key under the blotter—acknowledging it was probably the first place anyone would look—and walked over to the gilt-framed mirror on the wall where I stared at my reflection. My ordinary American face looked back at me. Why was I such a threat to someone here? How could a simple food publicity program, one of thousands being done on both sides of the Atlantic, cause such hatred?

Lucille, forget about British crime novels and consider that it could be just a practical joke. The British love practical jokes, jolly schoolboy humor. I fluffed up my hair, straightened my collar and smoothed the soft fabric of my dark red knitted dress over my hips. Good, the weight was staying off so far. I stood up straight, five feet nine, taller than most women, even if inches shorter than a supermodel.

Even if it was a practical joke, should I tell somebody? Should I call Barry in New York, or maybe Danny? Show the note to Jane or even confront Fiona?

Jane interrupted these thoughts by knocking and sticking her head in the door.

"Had a call from Will's secretary, the Lady Gillian. He wants to see us later this morning, as there have been some developments. He wants the press introduction delayed. He says he wants to wait until early August, he says the client isn't eager to start right away, he says . . ."

"I don't care what the great Will Hammersmith says. I want to stay on schedule. What's all this about the client not being eager? What client? I haven't laid eyes on the man yet to give him our plans. Why is Will doing this to us? What a bastard he is, trying to mess up the schedule we all agreed upon." I stopped to take a breath.

Jane's mouth had dropped open.

"Sorry, Jane. New York Office manners are obviously coarser than London's. Tell me, what's to stop me from making a quick visit this morning to the factory that churns out the dreaded Sweet Whippo? You told me it's on the north side of London. Can you make some arrangements for me? I need to see this wonder stuff actually being made and check it out thoroughly before I confront Will."

"This morning? But what shall I tell Gillian?" Jane's face broke into a grin. "I know, I'll tell her to tell him you've buggered off to the factory. That will get the wind up."

Her words stopped me cold. Could Jane, friendly Jane, have sent that nasty note to me?

"No, I'd best not pass the word along," she said, her face sobering. "Will Hammersmith is one of the power people around here. I suggest you postpone your visit to the factory until it is an official one. It doesn't pay to cross him."

"It doesn't pay to cross me either," I said firmly. I wanted her to spread the word around this office that I wasn't a pushover, even though I had given in to my stomach's demands yesterday. "My stomach is not really anxious to go to that factory this morning and watch that slimy stuff spew out of the machines. But before you call Gillian, can you tell me what the relationship is between Will and Fiona? They seem very close. Is she a power person, too?"

Jane sat down on the chair by my desk, apparently ready for a good gossip. "Word got round quickly that you and Fiona had an up-and-downer yesterday after you got sick at the tasting. Since you didn't suffer any permanent damage, I confess the whole thing made my day. It made the day for a few other people, too. Fiona has her supporters, but most of us resent her attitude. She treats me as if I know nothing about cookery except how to do bangers and mash. I'm told she has something going with Will, because he is eligible, you know. He was recently divorced and is up for grabs. Fiona gets around a lot socially. Some people think she's wonderful, what with all those glossy magazine articles she turns out and her showing up on the telly demonstrating how easy it is to cook those super meals. She *does* look good on the box," Jane said wistfully. "She knows her stuff, all right."

"Then why is she so determined to fight me every step of the way on this campaign?" I asked. "Of course she has her sainted reputation to consider while I am just the pushy American."

Jane got up from the chair. "I shouldn't have tattled to you. These offices could easily be bugged. But Fiona has made things bloody awful for me once in the past when I got in her way. Remind me to tell you about her and the Sweet Whippo client, but don't forget we need to see Mr. Hammersmith this morning. I'll get back to Gillian." She sailed out the door before I could stop her.

Yes, Fiona could definitely have sent that note. Apparently she was also someone who shouldn't be crossed. I sighed and pulled another stack of papers toward me, waiting for Jane's scheduling of the meeting with Will. Poisoned food, poison pen letters, Will trying to change our careful scheduling. So much for all the good times I had expected from my stint in London. If I were just going to survive these next six weeks I would have to grit my teeth and see this assignment through no matter *who* tried to do me in. Otherwise, it would be goodbye Lucille Anderson, Senior Vice President, MWVB, and hello New York State Unemployment Office. Or worse still, hello Hazelwood Haven, our family cemetery in Springfield, Missouri.

Chapter 5

Jane came in a few minutes later to say that Will had changed his mind and wanted just me for the meeting.

"What's up? Why just me?"

She shrugged, obviously relieved not to be in on the meeting. I started to ask her about her enigmatic comment on Fiona and the Sweet Whippo client, but she heard her phone ring, so turned and left quickly.

When I got to Will's office, Gillian, his secretary, suggested I take a chair and wait until the great man was free. I sat there, gazing at her perfectly streaked light brown hair, her glowing skin, more of those bright blue British eyes and listening to her upper-class accent. Jane had already explained to me that London Office was famous for its collection of girls from the best families working as secretaries and personal assistants until they married someone from another of the best families. One had even snagged a minor Royal. Gillian, like others I had seen here, looked like the girls in the photographs in the fancy *Queen* magazine or *Country Life*. They were nicknamed "Sloane Rangers" because of their patronage of exclusive shops on Sloane Street, their home territory. The personnel director, whom I had met briefly yesterday, was himself upper crust and according to Jane, crafty enough to hire the younger sons of the best titles to work here as a lure to get those classy secretaries. These young men she called "Chinless Wonders." Secretaries were harder to come by than the younger sons.

"Not terribly brainy, most of them, but they know all the right people," she had said. Gillian's disdainful look told me that in her books I was definitely not the right people.

She finally waved her well-manicured hand towards Will's office. I opened the door, stepped through and watched him go through the preliminaries of the smile, the coming out from behind his desk to seat me in a deep chair facing it. I was beginning to suspect that excessive politeness on the part of the British is an underhanded way to disarm you so that they can get their knives in faster. Had Will sent that nasty note?

I waited calmly for him to finish looking me over, his eyes sweeping me from head to toe. Today, I knew my suit was unwrinkled, my hair and nails sparkling, my shoes polished. Up for grabs, was he? Not by me. I looked back at him coolly.

"Jane tells me you want to do the press and media introduction later than we all, I emphasize *all*, had originally planned," I said, starting right in.

"Yes, I see no reason for all this rush. It's a simple launch, but I want to be sure we are totally organized," he said.

"And you think we aren't?"

"Fiona seems to feel . . ."

"Fiona may be the one who is not totally organized. She doesn't accept that there might be some drawbacks to her use of the product. You obviously heard that one of their recipes made me sick."

His barely suppressed smile told me that he had indeed heard about it. Fiona had probably had a wonderful time telling him about the ghastly noises from the loo in her quarters. "Nothing serious, I'm sure. Probably just a nervous stomach on your part, don't you know, what with jet lag and a new job."

"Did Fiona tell you why my so-called nervous stomach rebelled?"

"She said someone left the food out of the fridge overnight."

"Exactly. So how many of your British housewife consumers are going to have nervous stomachs, too, when they leave the food out overnight?"

That shook him.

"And another thing," I went on. "Half of the recipes are supposed to be American style and must be developed and tested right along with her British ones. Fiona and her staff can't seem to accept that."

"Fiona always knows what she's doing," he objected.

"And I don't?"

"Oh now, I didn't mean that."

"Then I see no reason to delay the launch. If Fiona would get her staff working on enough recipes, both British and American, and we got approval as soon as possible, then we can get on with the basic theme and work with the ad side to coordinate the whole launch. Back in New York, we always insist that publicity and advertising be closely coordinated."

I saw from his face that he hated to hear me say, "Back in New York."

"So," I went on, "unless you think your ad people can't cope with this, I suggest we stay on schedule. I don't want to be the one to have to tell Evan Jones that we are falling behind. Apparently this is a pet project of his." I knew Will wouldn't want to be the one, either, to give any bad news to the MWVB top man worldwide, but he didn't have to know that I had never laid eyes on this exalted personage, the World Chairman.

He swung around to the telephone. "Let's talk to Derek Land about this." He instructed Gillian to summon Derek, the account supervisor on the ad side for Sweet Whippo. I knew what Derek would have to say, as he had already tossed off a carefree comment during our brief introduction yesterday that he hadn't a clue about what he was supposed to be doing. An obvious chinless wonder man.

Will and I sat in silence, waiting for Derek, Will flicking through some papers, giving me the cold treatment for disagreeing with him. Outside the French windows I could see trees swaying gently in the square. London Office did not believe in stark, modern offices in dull, tall buildings convenient to a commuter railroad station. This office took up an entire building, a magnificent one, formerly the townhouse of a duke. It had high ceilings, tall windows, sweeping staircases and antique open cage elevators with polished brass grills to clang open and shut. The higher your status here, the lower the floor for your office. Will had his office on what is known as the first floor in Britain and Europe, which means second floor to us Americans. All the executive offices had antique furniture, good antique furniture. I had to agree that even my temporary office, although far less grand, was much nicer to work in than my glass-fronted open-plan office in New York, just one step up from a cubicle.

A discreet knock brought me out of my thoughts. It seemed Derek had dutifully arrived. But when the door opened, it was not Derek. Instead, a tall man, brown hair flecked with gray, and craggy features stood there.

"Brack! Didn't expect you today. Plans change or something? Thought you were on the Continent." Will stood up and walked quickly to the door.

"Gillian was not around, so I came through."

The man stood there and smiled at me, directly at me. I smiled back. Here was the best-looking man I'd seen in London Office, better looking than Will. Different looking.

Derek Land also stood in the doorway, slightly behind the man. I watched Will maneuver this "Brack" into the room while he shook his head at poor Derek and pushed him back, closing the door firmly in his startled face.

"Brack, you haven't had a chance to meet Lucille Anderson from our New York Office. She is in fact working on your Sweet Whippo account."

So this was *the* client, the elusive client who had been "off on the Continent." "Continent" was the buzz word in this office, instead of simply saying some country like France or Italy. But here he was in Will's office in person. Terrific news to me, as I much prefer dealing directly with a client instead of going through channels, so I can get faster approval or action. Maybe now things could actually get going.

"Braxton Clark," he said, holding out his hand. It was a warm, firm hand. "So you are the Yank helping us. Glad to have you. How are you finding it here?"

I forgave him the "Yank," which always makes me feel like a soldier in a World War I movie. I liked his hazel eyes, his strong features with a high-bridged nose, a wide mouth, even his graying hair. He looked to be around fifty. Of course I can never tell ages with Englishmen, because to me they either look around fifteen years old with their pink cheeks and schoolboy faces or fat and sixty with faces lined with little broken red veins.

"I'm very glad to meet you," I said, meaning it. "I'm finding it all a little dramatic, if you must know."

Will was hovering anxiously behind Braxton Clark and I could see that the wily man was planning to get rid of me as soon as possible. But he was going to run into problems trying to do that, as I wanted, yes, desperately needed, to talk to this client.

"Dramatic?" Clark asked. "Sounds interesting. Now that we're here, why don't we sit down and discuss the launch," he said, drawing up another chair, forcing Will to sit down, too. "I'm ready to talk Sweet Whippo."

I opened my mouth to begin, but Will cut me off.

"Brack, we're thinking about moving the launch date back a bit to give the kitchen a little more time to polish the recipes."

I shifted in my chair, barely containing myself.

Clark turned to me and asked, "Is this your idea?"

"No way. Of course we want to be absolutely sure that the recipes and their presentations are the best, but I'd like to keep as close to our original schedule as possible," I said firmly.

Clark kept a penetrating gaze on me for a moment, then turned back to Will.

"Why do *you* want to postpone the launch?"

Will smiled winningly. "We're having a tiny bit of a problem with our kitchen."

"The kitchen is actually having a tiny bit of a problem with Sweet Whippo," I said quickly.

I could feel Will's hostility flowing across that polished desk. Clark looked from Will to me, not smiling.

"Problem? I was told you were the expert on this kind of publicity program in the States."

"The problem is not with the publicity; the problem is with the recipes done so far and possible trouble with lack of refrigeration. Even allergic reactions should be considered."

The silence was not reassuring.

"But I think these problems can be worked out," I went on quickly. "New recipes for both British and American food can be done right away, and we can make sure we know what we're doing with this product and stay on schedule. In fact, now that you are on the premises, Mr. Clark, we can work even faster."

"Then you see no reason to delay the launch, Miss Anderson?"

"No. I'm all for keeping right on schedule."

"Then I say we should stay on the same schedule," Clark said quietly. "Leave any product problems to me, but Sweet Whippo has been analyzed, tested, retested, stored and shelved and tried out in freezers, fridges, cookers and microwaves, even barbecue pits. There should be no physical problem at all with this product."

Will shrugged and leaned back in his chair, but his hands were gripping the arms of that chair hard. I knew I would pay later for my open rebellion.

Clark turned to Will. "I also need to know how the campaign is going on the advertising side. Are we still following the same approach? When I checked into my office this morning, there wasn't much from you, Will, and that's why I decided to come by."

Will's face flushed. "It's early days yet, but of course, we'll get on it right away."

Clark went on. "Why don't we have everyone on the account meet with me as soon as possible? How about tomorrow?"

I thought Will's hands would rip the arms off the chair, but he recovered quickly. "Er, no, tomorrow is actually a bit inconvenient as I have to be away from the office, in fact, over the weekend. Complicated plans, hard to break, as much as I'd like to. Tell you what, how about next week? Monday all right?"

Clark's face didn't look like Monday was all right, but after some thought, he nodded. "In the meantime, why don't you and I talk about these problems, Miss Anderson? Can't get the campaign off the ground if the recipes don't work. I hate to think of the problems if consumers buy our product and then don't like what they can or can't do with it."

Not to mention the possibility of consumers all over Britain throwing up, I almost said, but clamped my mouth shut. Will's face was stony after this last remark of Clark's.

I stood up. "If you could come with me now to my office, we could make a start, Mr. Clark."

He promptly stood up and walked over to stand by me. He was at least half a head taller than I, and I got a good whiff of his aftershave lotion. Was this Englishman single? No, of course he was married. Every interesting-looking man his age was bound to have a "lady wife" in her garden or else be married to one of these intelligent, articulate, stunning women whom I'd seen on talk shows or profiled in the *Times* and *Telegraph*. Or he could be gay. I sighed.

"Bad as that, is it?" Clark asked.

Sharp observer, Lucille. Obviously not your usual product manager with sales and bottom-line-only attitude. He could be fun to work with.

Will ushered us both out the door, all smiles with Clark, but when Clark turned his back, he gave me a look that meant there was vengeance ahead for me.

Chapter 6

I led Braxton Clark up one flight of stairs and down the hall to my own office. When he had settled himself in the chair by my desk, I handed him several of the initial recipes from Fiona's kitchen staff, including the one that had made me sick.

"Before we get to some of the product problems, perhaps you could look at these and tell me what you think." My voice was deliberately matter-of-fact.

He glanced at them quickly, raised eyebrows at one, nodded at another and then handed them back to me.

"I see what you mean. But new recipes can certainly be devised easily enough. What I'd like to know is what kind of launch you think would work best in Britain. I'd like some input from your American experience." He was serious, but ended the sentence with a smile. I liked him even more. I could work with this client. Closely, I hoped. Very closely.

I told him, "The media are changing so fast over here that I can't quite keep up—new newspapers, cable and satellite television, not to mention online activity—so I have to leave that to Jane Mallow and this office. What we found that worked in America was to get some really good recipes and product uses together, do black and white and color photography for the print media; do some videos or CDs for television, politely known as infomercials; record similar cassettes for radio, even a video or two if necessary, and then bring it all together with a nice big media launch. A luncheon, preferably, where a range of dishes could be featured and actually tasted by the power people in the food world. Then we took the same format to a second big city and so on. I think the same thing will work over here. But everything depends upon presenting some recipes showing how Sweet Whippo can be used to produce really good dishes and why it should be used instead of fat, salt, and sugar. Of course in the U.S. we coordinated our launch with the advertising side so that when we went into a city the ads had already shown up in the local newspapers and on the radio and television. That meant that people in the area had already seen and heard about the product. If the ads had done their work, those people were interested in knowing more. I think something similar will work well here, too, especially if you follow the London press launch with similar ones in, say, Birmingham and Edinburgh, maybe Bristol and Dublin." I took a big breath and sat back.

He leaned nearer, watching me closely, and I started getting nervous. But I looked him straight in the eye and kept calm. He was so close I could see that his eyes were definitely hazel. Little flecks of gold in them. He smelled wonderful and I could recognize Penhaligon Cologne, now one of my new favorites.

Jane knocked politely on my door and then came in with a sheaf of papers in her hand. She stopped abruptly when she saw Braxton Clark.

"Oh dear, I am sorry, Mr. Clark, I didn't realize you were here." She was obviously flustered as she handed me the papers. "Fiona just sent these new recipes by hand, wanted your opinion right away, Lucille. She says they have an American slant."

Clark stood up and greeted her politely and she turned to go back to her office.

"Wait a minute, Jane, you should be in on this meeting." I turned to Braxton, expecting his approval.

But he surprised me by saying, "If you don't mind, Jane, I'd like to get to know Miss Anderson here, what she thinks, how she works, before we all work together. Do you mind?"

Jane shook her head politely, murmured excuses and departed, giving me a lifted eyebrow on her way out.

Clark sat down again.

"Please call me Lucille," I said. "Americans are a little more informal."

"It's Brack, short for Braxton," he said, and reached out his hand. We shook again, only this time he held my hand a little longer than necessary.

I took a deep breath, held out the pages of recipes and we obediently looked over this new lot, his head even closer to mine. I was glad I had on plenty of my favorite perfume, "Pleasures." Seemed appropriate.

The first recipe, Praline Blanc, called for meringue baskets filled with ground pecans; the second masterpiece was Courgette Quiche, which translated into zucchini and eggs; and the third one was Roast Beef with Red-currant Sauce.

I tried to be diplomatic, but when he looked up at me, I couldn't help saying, "True blue American recipes, wouldn't you say? I wonder what happened to the Lemon Chiffon Pie and Corn Pudding and Barbecued Beef I put in my notes."

He laughed and shook his head. "I think Fiona needs a little direction from you. In fact, a lot of direction."

"There are other problems, too." I took a breath and told him about my bout with unrefrigerated Sweet Whippo and asked delicately about possible allergic reactions.

He was definitely upset. He jumped to his feet and started pacing around, telling me that hundreds of tests had been done on the product—tests for allergic reactions—and for necessary refrigeration, and all had shown absolutely no problems.

"Let's go talk to Fiona right now," I suggested. I wanted her to see that this client and I were working very, very closely together and that he would back me up.

"Right. Let's do just that," he agreed.

Jane chose this moment to knock and come in again. "Mr. Clark is wanted on the telephone, I'm afraid. Would you like to take it in here?"

He nodded, grimacing slightly, so I diplomatically followed Jane back to her adjoining office, closing the door behind me firmly.

"Couldn't resist taking another look at him," she admitted. "He's dishy. Remind me to tell you about Fiona and Braxton Clark."

"Tell me now."

But she shook her head and said, "Later. It's really only gossip."

Before I could pounce on her, Clark opened the door. "Sorry about that. I'm afraid I'll have to leave Fiona to you. Bit of a problem at the plant."

Damn, now I would have to battle her on my own again.

I walked him down the hall to our antique elevator and when the cage lift arrived, he pulled open the metal gates, turned and shook my hand very businesslike, then startled me by asking if I were free for a quick drink or two at the Connaught after work, say six o'clock, so we could finish knocking some of the ideas about. "The back bar, if you could come."

I stammered, "Of course, of course," as he clanged shut

the grillwork and the cage started disappearing from sight. I stood there at the very edge of the lift, watching him looking up at me through the open top bars as he descended. I was glad I had on my best lacy underwear.

Apparently even the lace didn't help much, because at the end of the day, I got a message from my secretary that Clark had called and said he was very sorry but that he had to cancel the invitation. He would get back to me soon.

When I got to Fiona's kitchen to tell her about my talk with client Braxton Clark, she didn't even give me a chance. All I got was a quick hello and goodbye. "Must fly," she said, brushing by me, a smile on her face and out the door before I could stop her. I heard her shoes clicking on the hard floor and the door closing quickly.

When I turned back, there was Pauline with a smug look on her face. "She's off to Paris with Mr. Hammersmith. There *are* other accounts besides Sweet Whippo, you know. Fiona is very much in demand."

I made Pauline pay for that by spending an hour going over American ideas for Sweet Whippo, pounding my ideas into her stubborn head. Turkey à la King, Candied Sweet Potatoes, Pork Chops in Gravy. She cooperated, but sulkily, and kept shaking her head, that straw-colored hair falling in her face. The other women on the staff were nowhere to be seen and I guessed they were making themselves scarce.

Later, when I reported Pauline's words about Fiona being much in demand back to Jane, I got a good guffaw from her. "I'll say so. Fiona demands very much herself, or so I'm told. Sit down, Lucille, and I will fill you in on the gossip. I think you should know what is going on, or has gone on. Apparently Braxton Clark and Fiona had quite a fling last year. They were working together on another product from his company. It's a big conglomerate, you know. Then I heard that affair was no longer going on, but that she had taken on Will Hammersmith. Your mouth is open, Lucille. Surely these things go on in New York Office."

"Of course, of course. What I really want to know is, is Braxton Clark available, then?"

"Divorced and available, so far as I know. Why? Are you interested?"

"Might be."

"Do it. If I weren't already promised to my Jeremy, I'd try. But I'd be careful, as Fiona would not take lightly to your seeing him socially even though they're supposed to be through. I've heard she can be rough. Probably stamp you to death with those spike heels she wears." Jane laughed briefly at her own wit and started walking toward the door. "I'll give you another chapter sometime, but right now, I'm off to the No. 74 bus or I'm in trouble with Jeremy."

The next day was Friday, the last day of my first three work days in London Office. I approached my desk with trepidation, dreading to see another of those little buff envelopes, but the desktop was clean. Yes, it must have been just a practical joke. Jane was not around to talk to; she was at an all-day seminar on another account that didn't involve me. Pauline was busy with her staff, working on the recipes that Fiona had to present on Monday at the big meeting for Sweet Whippo.

"Fiona wants everyone to see what super dishes we can make," Pauline told me when I went down to the kitchen later in the morning to check on progress. "We'll give everyone a taste next Monday."

"American ones better be on that table," I said.

"Of course, of course," Pauline said.

"Shall I come back down when some are ready?"

"Oh no. Fiona insists that absolutely no one see or taste any recipes before the big meeting. She'll come in on Sunday, after she gets back from Paris, for the final approval."

"On Sunday?"

"Fiona is dedicated to her work," was the smug reply. "She insists on being all alone to taste each one. Very serious. I'll work Saturday, you know, to make sure all is right."

I couldn't budge her and after hearing a few more paragraphs on the joys of working with Fiona, I gave up. I took a long, long lunch hour spent wandering through Harvey Nichols and Peter Jones and Harrods, looking at leather handbags. No word from Braxton Clark. I really wanted to call and give a brief report to Barry back in New York City. Oh, we'd been communicating these last days with brief E-mail messages and a couple of faxes, but I had been careful with what I had said—made no mention of food poisoning or nasty notes—because too many eyes watch both. Then I thought better of it and changed my mind about calling New York. What had I accomplished in my time in London? Nothing to brag about. I had received a nasty anonymous note, had been given a serious stomachache by the test kitchen, as well as having war declared on me and my American ideas by Fiona Gordon. And Will Hammersmith tried to delay the launch, probably arranging to have me recalled to New York. That Senior Vice President title began to fade into the distance. The only good thing that had happened was Braxton Clark and even he had also faded. Now what would next week bring?

What the next week brought was death.

Chapter 7

I walked back slowly to the flat on Friday evening. I didn't spot anyone following me; in fact, the neighborhood seemed deserted, with everybody off having a great time somewhere without me. Fiona and Will were in Paris, Braxton Clark was probably having a dirty weekend at a riverside inn with Lady somebody or other; even Jane had said she and her Jeremy were going hill walking. The weekend stretched ahead of me. Yes, I was in my favorite city, yes, I was on an expense account, and yes, I could do as I pleased. But yes, I was homesick. I telephoned Danny and got his answering machine. I telephoned my parents and got their answering machine. The final insult was when I turned on the television and there, in glorious color and wraparound sound, was Fiona, surrounded by handsome people, all celebrities unknown to me, all of them laughing and talking and daintily tasting gourmet dishes. Had Pauline deliberately lied to me about Fiona going to Paris with Will? Suddenly, I felt that everyone in London had been lying to me all week. I had to admit that Fiona did a terrific job on television, prancing around in yet another beautiful dress—this one a black-and-pink print with those shiny black pumps with stiletto heels, Fiona's "signature," dear Pauline had told me this afternoon, pointedly looking down at my comfortable flats. Secretly, I envied Fiona's stylish feet. Mine were too fat to cram into fashionable high-heeled shoes because I ended up looking like I had on Minnie Mouse pumps. I poured myself a drink. I was too tired to go out to any of the glittering attractions London held. I went to bed early, wondering why I was putting myself through all this. That Senior Vice Presidency had lost its appeal. But I needed my job.

When I woke up in the morning, it was raining, which made my mood even darker. I didn't want to admit how low I felt to Danny, so I didn't call him again for fear he would say I told you so. To shake myself out of this mood, I made myself go out of the flat, take the No. 74 bus to Harvey Nichols, where I bought a sweater and treated myself to a good, if expensive, lunch. When the rain let up, I bused back to Leicester Square where I stood in line at the TKTS booth, picked out a good play for later that evening, stopped by Tesco's Oxford Street supermarket and stocked up on my comfort foods—peanut butter, ice cream, brownies—and picked up some English foods—lamb chops and smoked Scottish salmon.

To make myself do something constructive, I took out my manuscript, that mystery I was writing, and made several pages of notes on the changes in the English character I had noted on television so I could bring the novel up to date. I sat in front of my laptop, hands poised over the keys, trying to write. Nothing came into my mind but nasty notes, Sweet Whippo and Braxton Clark. I put away the laptop and ate supper in front of the television, taxied down later to the theater and enjoyed it thoroughly. It helped my homesickness. On Sunday morning, Danny called me, swore he missed me, but smothered a laugh when I decided to tell him how I'd gotten sick in the test kitchen from spoiled food made with Sweet Whippo. For some reason, I still didn't tell him about the note. I don't know why.

"You can't take getting sick off that stuff seriously, Lucy," he told me. "It was just an accident. You know you've told me before that it's a wonder people don't puke more from some of the recipes test kitchens dream up. Don't worry; it will all work out. I do miss you, but I know this a good career move for you."

He sounded pompous and not at all sympathetic, but talking to him did cheer me up. Danny had been my lover for five years and he couldn't help it if I wasn't sure I wanted to marry him. He was good looking, with dark curly hair and a sardonic smile and easy to be with, too easy, maybe. But, I'm here and he's there, so I left the flat and rode the bus to Covent Garden to watch the jugglers and street performers. I love riding on those big red buses because I can sit up top and watch London and its population as the buses lumber through the streets. I even took a ride on the London Eye—the big ferris wheel. Eventually I forgot the week's past events, and I rode back to the flat in a good humor again, optimistic about the coming week.

I was particularly pleased when I got upstairs and found a glossy shopping bag—called a carrier bag over here—on the hall table. See, somebody did love me—obviously a present from Danny via his credit card. Inside was a small, elegant box of chocolates. I snatched at the card enclosed. This one said, "Eat Me If You Dare!" No signature. That Danny! Teasing me about my food poisoning! I called him to thank him.

"No, Lucy, I didn't send them. I thought about sending flowers to cheer you up, but never quite got around to it. Must be one of your new friends." He sounded a bit guilty.

Suddenly, I was worried. Really worried. Did that message, "Eat Me If You Dare!" mean that these wonderful chocolates had been poisoned? I stared at the rows of luscious, heart-breaking, gorgeous truffles. Dark, bittersweet chocolate, rolled in cocoa, my very favorite. My hand trembled as I picked up one. God, I wanted that piece; I could practically taste it, the smooth flavor rolling around in my mouth, on my tongue. What kind of twisted mind sends someone a box of chocolates and includes a note like that, daring me to eat them? Fiona, that's who, I thought immediately. Her type of practical joke. First, poisoned desserts and now poisoned chocolates. Shades of Agatha Christie. But, I remembered how sick I'd been in the test kitchen and that made me too apprehensive to try even one truffle. I put the piece back, closed the box firmly, put it in the freezer, away from temptation, with the thought that I could have the contents analyzed next week on the quiet and then see if I were paranoid or just cautious. Or, maybe it was Will's way of getting back at me for taking the client Braxton Clark away from his office. Yes, he could have done something like this.

I went downstairs and asked the hall porter how the candy had been delivered.

"By messenger, Madam. I assumed it was from the shop round the corner because of the carrier bag. I recognized it."

"A woman didn't bring them here personally?"

He was puzzled at my question and wrinkled his brow in thought. "A delivery lad handed the carrier bag to me, and I sent Charles with it upstairs." Charles was his ever-obliging assistant. "That was this afternoon about half two." He looked at me sharply, obviously wondering why I was so concerned.

"But it wasn't necessarily the delivery boy from the shop?" I persisted.

"I can't say for certain, Madam."

He must have thought I was making a big deal out of a box of chocolates. I gave up and went back up to the flat, where I checked the label on the box, looked up the telephone number of the shop and called them, only to be told by a snippy salesperson that they never gave out the names of their customers, and they had no record of a delivery to my address. No amount of my sharp questioning changed his mind. He implied that a person of my obvious lower class should just be grateful indeed to receive a box of *their* exalted chocolates. So much for my razor-sharp questioning and detecting. I was batting zero trying to be a detective. I decided I was damned if I would tell anybody on either side of the Atlantic Ocean about this latest slap in the face. I would indeed take them to a lab and have them tested, though, and woe to London Office if they turned out to have been tampered with! Then I would blab it all over two continents.

The meeting the next day was so much on my mind that I worked the whole evening and well into the night going over plans and recipes. I did not want to appear stupid about British food terms, particularly in front of Braxton Clark, so I taught myself that jacket potato meant baked potato, double cream meant whipping cream, jelly for gelatin, cooker for stove, hob for burner, gateau for cake, tin for can, marrow for zucchini, aubergine for eggplant, mange tout for sugar snaps, (I couldn't see myself asking for mange tout at the A&P back home) and even tried to sort out the sugars: castor sugar, icing sugar, demerara, rainbow and even more. I dreamed of food all night. I even dreamed that I ate those chocolates and survived.

The next morning, all the MWVB staff assigned to

Sweet Whippo had dutifully assembled at nine a.m. in the boardroom when I got there, most of them grumbling at the early hour. All except Fiona, who must have been planning a spectacular entrance. Unlike New York, London Office did not insist upon staff coming in early, as that smacked of working class hours, and so the executives rarely got in before nine-thirty. Jane had complained, delicately, that she *had* noticed more and more people coming in earlier, American style. Everything bad gets blamed on America, I told her delicately. The boardroom had been a drawing room in the duke's original mansion, and its high and decorated ceilings were set off by an ornate chandelier. In the center of the room was a twenty-foot long Regency-style table with a highly polished mahogany surface. The requisite writing pads and sharpened pencils were neatly set at each place. There was coffee in silver pots on the elegant sideboard, together with china cups—no Styrofoam containers here—and we helped ourselves and stood chatting.

Already in position on a side table was an elaborate spread of four cold desserts made with Sweet Whippo. Each had a table tent with its title and the facts: how much less fat, salt and sugar than prepared the traditional way, plus the so-called nutritional benefit of using Sweet Whippo—no cholesterol and full of great fiber. I checked to be sure there were American choices included and spotted a pumpkin pie, and an apple pie. Good God, it had a pastry swan perched atop it. Did I imagine it or were the sidelong looks from the group given to the display full of apprehension? Was there really something weird about this new product Sweet Whippo?

When one man caught me watching him as he looked at the display, he smiled and shook his head ruefully. At least he didn't cut his throat in the sign language that I saw another man do.

Pauline bustled about putting out warming trays and instructing her minions as to the exact minute to bring out the hot dishes from the adjoining kitchen as soon as the first part of the meeting was over. Fiona apparently didn't bother herself with manual labor. She was probably putting the final touches on her grooming. I thought again about the chocolates and gritted my teeth. Don't let yourself show any anger and yes, Lucille, fear. Plain old fear. Somebody was playing nasty games with me.

Will Hammersmith waited impatiently during the coffee chatter and then asked us all to sit down at the long table to wait for the client. Braxton Clark showed up right on time. He greeted those whom he knew by name, smiled at me, nodded at the introductions and then took a quick look at the dishes on the sideboard. He made no comment about them.

"Are we all here? Where's Fiona?"

Pauline assured him Fiona was on her way.

Braxton frowned but sat down. Will took over then. He went carefully over the agenda, got capsule reports from as many individuals as he could, complimented Pauline on the test kitchen's prowess and said he was looking forward to the tastings.

"Now, how about our Yank contingent?"

I knew Will had done that "Yank" bit on purpose, but I ignored it and started right in doing my show-and-tell routine. The show was a little sparse, just a few sample press releases and three of our best photographs from the Goodsauce promotion in the U.S. to explain the kind of photography I wanted to do. The tell part was better as I outlined the kind of media introduction we'd like to offer.

The hours I had put it on it last night paid off. I kept it brief, waiting to use the real ammunition on Brack later and in person.

Will listened, unsmiling, and kept looking at his watch. He nodded when I finished, said, "Right, right, that will have to do."

Jane added her facts and figures on the schedules of photography and releases, sounding very knowledgeable. She was learning fast, that girl. Derek Land, with his pink-cheeked face appearing perplexed, waffled on so much and gave so few real facts that it was obvious to all that very little had actually been done on the ad side. Will frowned, cut him off abruptly and started in on the media crew. They gave the usual pitch with figures and market sectors, ratings, classes, upmarket and downmarket publications and radio/TV media. Pauline and her staff took away the dirty cups, put carafes of water and crystal glasses on the table. She added a centerpiece of anemones, glorious in their blue and red colors. I made a note to see if I could swipe the centerpiece afterwards on some pretext of photo styling ideas.

We all stood up and stretched, then sat down at the table like good little children, ready for hot food, followed by our just desserts. Instead, Pauline started serving small plates of desserts. I certainly wouldn't have begun a food tasting with desserts, but obviously Fiona was pulling rank and sticking to her idea that Sweet Whippo belonged in sweet foods. Pauline was in her element here, as she and her assistants laid out samples in sequence in front of each of us with the appropriate silver forks and spoons and cobalt blue rimmed china plates. No plastic forks to desecrate her offerings. During the silence that followed, we all dutifully chewed and swallowed. Nobody actually retched, which was a plus;

55

in fact, most of the desserts, even the American ones, tasted fine. Sweet Whippo was doing its part. We all watched Braxton Clark surreptitiously as he tasted the offerings.

"American enough for you?" he asked as he turned to me, finally.

"Need a little work, but a good start, I think." Very diplomatic of me.

He nodded. "Agreed. Now let's get on with the campaign as soon as possible. I have a few facts and figures to give to this group when these bits get cleared away and the hot food brought in." He looked around. "Fiona here yet?" he asked.

Will said, "Probably in the kitchen checking the food."

As the dishes were removed from the table, I joined the others as we all stood up to stretch again. This meeting seemed interminable. Brack kept a steady eye on me, and I was glad I had worn my newest outfit of dark green linen suit with pale yellow shirt. I'd even put on beige pumps with medium heels. Then the outside door opened and a sober-faced man beckoned to Will.

I watched Will walk to the door, then turn and signal to Pauline, who rushed over. He said something to her and Pauline's quickly stifled outburst gained the attention of everyone in the room instantly, as we all turned our heads to watch the scene.

Will's face was noticeably ashy and set when he turned to face us all.

"It's Fiona."

He waited a moment and then added. "There's been an accident."

We waited.

"She's dead, I'm afraid."

After an audible intake of breath from the assembled

group, a brief silence fell.

Braxton Clark was the first to break it to say, "Good God. Accident? What was it? Car crash? How?"

"Apparently she fell down the steps at her flat last night or early this morning, when they found her. Broke her neck," Will said calmly.

The shock went right through me. As the room erupted into murmurs, I couldn't quite take the situation in. I had this mental picture of Fiona falling down a long flight of stairs, head over those spiky high heels. I shook my head to clear it, but I couldn't manage to say anything.

I heard Will's voice as he quieted the group saying, "If it's all right with you, Brack, I think we'd best adjourn this meeting now. This is a sad affair. But will you come with me to my office?"

Braxton nodded and looked over at me; I sensed that he wanted me to join them. Will caught the look and put his hand on his arm.

"We need a word in private."

The sober-faced man, whom nobody had bothered to introduce, joined them, and they spoke for a minute. I couldn't hear what was said and I moved a little closer. Braxton looked at me again and shook his head ruefully. He mouthed the word "later," so I had to be content with that as I watched the trio of men depart. I stood around for a while, listening to more shocked comments, then went over to talk to Pauline. She was sitting down at the table, looking straight forward, her round, placid face pale. I murmured my sympathies and she laid her hand on my arm and started to say something, then turned back and put her head in her hands. I sat down in a chair beside her. Finally, one of her staff touched her on the shoulder and then helped her up and out the door. I had a brief pang of guilt about my treatment of Fiona. But how could I know she was going to die?

Then I callously thought about the Sweet Whippo campaign and wondered what Fiona's death would mean. Would the program go on? Of course it would, but there would be a delay while things were rearranged. I felt guilty again thinking about work while Fiona lay dead. Jane signaled that we should leave and we did, walking silently back to the Public Relations offices, where we told the various staff the news.

When I finally got to my own office and opened the door, I saw it right away. Another little buff envelope was lying on my desk. Not now, I thought. This is too much.

This one said, "You were warned. Now bugger off fast!"

Chapter 8

That did it. Two such shocks in one day were too much. I picked up the note, crammed it into my handbag and walked into Jane's office.

"I'm going home. If Braxton Clark calls, give him my home number." I started for the door.

"Are you all right, Lucille? You look a bit pale." Then she caught herself and said, "Wise of you, very wise. Quite a shock."

I didn't answer. Somehow I couldn't answer. Who could be sending me these nasty notes? Surely not Jane, but now I was beginning to suspect everyone. Who could be so callous as to add this insult to the horror of the news about Fiona's death? I couldn't quite believe she was dead. When I read—and wrote about death in my mystery novel—it all seemed so simple and unemotional. But here was a woman I knew and had worked with and suddenly she was dead of a broken neck.

A light but persistent drizzle was coming down as I walked the few blocks to the flat, but I welcomed the coolness on my face and hair. It was good to get outside, away from that elegant townhouse of offices with the buzz of conversation about Fiona and her death. I had barely got inside my door when the telephone rang. It was Brack.

"I heard you went home in shock. Are you all right?"

"I guess so. I just can't take it all in. Poor Fiona."

"Terrible thing to happen. Terrible. We must talk. Can you have lunch with me if you feel up to it?"

"Yes, of course. I'm not sick, just upset." I wanted to add, "Getting another threatening note didn't help," but I didn't.

"I'll pick you up at one."

I hung up the phone, considerably cheered. Then it rang again. This time it was Will.

"Heard you weren't well, very pale, Jane said. We must talk. Lunch all right?"

"No, I can't make that, I really can't."

"Then later. I'll come by the flat. How about six o'clock? Will you be feeling better then? It's very important."

He sounded unstoppable, so I assured him I would. Jane must be telling everyone she saw that I was in trauma. I had this sinking feeling Will was going to drop a bomb on me about canceling the whole campaign now that Fiona was dead. I must work on Brack to prevent this. I didn't want to go back to New York City. I wanted to stay here. I told myself it was because I wanted to find out who had sent me those notes and who had sent me the chocolates and were they the same person? I also admitted to myself I didn't want to leave Brack.

Then the telephone rang again and this time it was Pauline. She sounded strange, her voice so strangled that I could hardly understand her.

"Lucille, I must talk to you. It's about Fiona. Nobody will believe me, nobody, but maybe you can help me. Fiona was murdered, I just know she was."

After I found my voice I asked, "Pauline, why are you saying this? I heard it was a tragic accident." Pauline's dramatic announcement then started me thinking. After my food poisoning and those nasty notes, even the chocolates, maybe Fiona had been a victim herself, a victim of murder?

Pauline went on and I listened carefully to her.

"No it wasn't an accident. I can't tell you over the telephone, but you must help me. Can we meet somewhere right now?"

"I can't make it so soon, I'm really sorry." I thought quickly and said, "Later, maybe, around four, if that's all right. Come by here for tea." I hoped that would soothe her.

But no, she started crying and talking and I couldn't follow what she was saying, something about telephone calls and stairs and a man in a big car. Finally she got enough control of her voice to agree she would come here because I was the only one who could help her.

When I put the telephone down, I took a very deep breath. Then I sat on the floor, crossed my legs in the yoga half lotus posture, closed my eyes and took more deep breaths. When my brain had calmed, I said aloud, "Lucille, think about this very carefully. You wanted material for your mystery novel and you've got enough here for two books, what with threatening notes, possible poisoned chocolates, that bout in the test kitchen and now the death of a colleague. This is real life, though, not fiction. These are things that are actually happening to *you,* a death of someone you worked with. Maybe you should just go back to the New York office."

"What should I do?" I asked myself. I often talk out loud because it clears my head.

I thought a bit and then I said, "Lucille, you could just listen to Pauline, to hear why she thinks Fiona was murdered. Then, make up your mind if you think you are competent enough to get involved in a murder investigation. It could be dangerous, because somebody out there has already made it plain that he or she is playing for keeps. If you get mixed up in an investigation, you may well regret it."

"The least I can do is listen to the poor girl," I said in a properly sympathetic voice as I rose, not too gracefully, from the rug and headed for the shower. What I really meant was that there was no way I was going to throttle my curiosity when I had a chance to be part of all this. And then there was Brack.

When I was in the shower, letting the hot water cascade over me, my mind jumping around from Pauline to Fiona to Will to Brack to Sweet Whippo and the thought that I might be heading back to New York sooner than I wanted, I had a truly inspired idea about the Sweet Whippo campaign.

Brack showed up at my door right on time, took my hand and held it.

"You're sure you're up to this?" he asked, peering closely at me.

"Yes, I'm much, much better," I said. His hand was warm and firm. I didn't want to let go, but I finally did after I dragged him into the flat and offered him a drink.

"No drink, but I will look around," he said. "Heard it was fancy, and my company no doubt footed part of the bill." He opened doors and peered into the bedroom and kitchen, then turned around and smiled. "Looks comfortable enough to me. Let's be off. The restaurant is just a few blocks away and the walk will do you good, buck up your spirits."

I smiled to myself. You'd think I'd collapsed in a heap back in the office the way everyone had become so solicitous. But of course he didn't know about the notes. Or did he?

I wanted to start right in asking him about what he had learned about Fiona's death, but decided to throttle my curiosity until later.

There was still a light rain, but he held me close to him as we sheltered under his large umbrella and walked slowly to the restaurant. It was a quiet, sternly elegant place with a subdued tinkle of glass and china and murmur of conversation. We were seated at a table tucked into a corner. The vase of anemones in the center reminded me briefly of the big bowl of those same bright blooms that had graced the long table in the boardroom this morning and I shook my head to get rid of the image of that man coming to the door to tell Will about Fiona's death. I found I was hungry— after all, we had only had a brief chance to sample those cold desserts—but I decided against eating too much so I could get some more attention for my delicate sensibilities. It felt good to be looked after. I passed up an appetizer but watched Brack eat his soup as I sipped my white wine. I was waiting for just the right moment to spring my new Sweet Whippo campaign on him. Public Relations Rule No. 1: Timing is everything with a client. I also wanted desperately to find out what he knew about Fiona's death. I didn't dare mention Pauline's telephone call about murder when I asked him what was new in the sad case of Fiona.

"The police consider it straightforward, according to Reid, that Detective Inspector who came along to tell us. They believe she tripped on those steps leading up to her flat. They are steep and marble, lethal stuff. Broke her neck instantly."

He'd been on those steps, had he? Perhaps once too often. Lucille, stop it. Stop playing detective. He went on, after giving me a sharp look. Had my face shown something?

"Her downstairs neighbor found her there this morning, but she had been dead since last night, the police figured. There will be an autopsy, of course." He grimaced and sat quietly for a moment, his eyes focused on something far, far away. Then he shook himself and said, "Poor Fiona."

"You knew her well?"

He looked at me carefully, the hazel eyes narrowed.

"I see the office grapevine has already been at work. Yes, I knew her well, last year it was, but I haven't seen much of her lately, except at your offices." He kept his gaze on me and I tried to look unconcerned.

"How was she dressed?" I asked, the image of Fiona's body lying crumpled at the foot of the stairs all night long burned into my mind.

"What?"

"I mean, was she in those high heels and a dress or was she in pants and low heels?"

He was obviously startled. "Why do you ask?"

"Just wondered how it could happen. Was she walking downstairs to go out or was she coming back home?"

He looked at me sharply, then shook his head again. "If you must know, they said she was in pants, her hostess pants, I think she called them, the kind with the big legs, and she did have on those spiky heeled shoes she always wore. The police say she might have caught her heel in the pants."

"I've done that very thing," I said, shivering. "Those wide-bottom pants can really trip you. She couldn't have been going out in that outfit, so why was she on the stairs?" I thought about it for a moment, then added, "Oh, I know, she was probably seeing a guest out, was standing at the top of the steps. But I'm surprised no one heard her fall, not even the guest, who couldn't have been too far away when she turned to go back into her flat." I then pictured said guest giving her a shove and running down the stairs and out the door.

Brack looked down at his plate, studying it. Then when he finally looked up at me, I thought *he* looked a bit pale. "Why are you so interested in this? It's downright ghoulish."

"No, it's not. I need facts so I can fix it in my mind, not keep wondering about her fall. I have a vivid imagination and I definitely need to get the right picture in my mind." Would he accept this weak excuse?

He studied me for a full minute but apparently accepted my explanation before he went on. "There was an older woman who lives in the ground floor flat but she apparently had her television on full blast and didn't hear anything. There are also people in the two flats above Fiona but they were away for the weekend."

"Is that what Detective Inspector Reid told you?" I boldly asked.

"That's what he said to us both. Now they want Will to represent the agency in the inquiry. Technically, he's her boss. But let's not talk about Fiona any more. We all are sorry for her, so young and with a great career ahead." He dropped his eyes, sighed, and then looked up and said, "Let's talk about you."

I wanted to find out what more the police had to say about the death, but I thought it better to drop it, so I smiled and said, "I've got a better idea. Let's talk about Sweet Whippo, but not until I've eaten. I'm starved. Please wait because I've got this new plan, which you may or may not like. Be perfectly frank, but I think it may just work."

I had to break off to admire the way the waiter deftly filleted the Dover sole I had ordered, removing the backbone with all the skill of a surgeon. The fish was surrounded with piped potatoes and those tiny, tiny sweet peas England produces. I waited hungrily but patiently until Brack was served his roast veal. I did not even mention Sweet Whippo while we both devoured our meals and discussed the finer points of the dishes and the wines with them. He knew good food, all right. Pre-Sweet Whippo.

"Feeling better?" he asked with a raised eyebrow as he looked over at my empty plate where not a morsel of food was left to be seen.

"Much, much better. In fact, I think I'll have something chocolaty for dessert, sorry, pudding. Comfort food, we call it. I'm wild for chocolate, you know."

"I didn't know, but I'll make sure to remember," he said with a grin.

So he wasn't the one who sent me the chocolates. Why had I even suspected him? I suspected everybody in Great Britain these days and after all, I knew very little about Braxton Clark except that he had had an affair with Fiona. Could they have been together in this plot to get rid of good old Lucille? I shook my head to clear it, took a deep breath and then did my best public relations presentation of the brand new Sweet Whippo campaign.

"How do you feel about having a Sweet Whippo cook-off, so to speak, between an American chef and a British chef? A friendly contest to see which country can produce the best recipes with this new product, a contest which will be judged by the media food experts at our press introduction luncheon? That way, we could make it sort of a memorial to Fiona, a special recognition of her work in the food field, and we wouldn't need to use any of our test kitchen's recipes, which are only half done, anyway."

I stopped abruptly. "I don't think I'm presenting this very well."

He laughed and said, "I think I get what you are saying. We can go on with the campaign without seeming to be cold-blooded about Fiona's death."

"Am I cold-blooded?"

"No, I wouldn't say so. Practical, maybe."

"There's a lot at stake," I protested. "It seems a shame to junk the whole campaign, when so much money has already been put into it. And I've seen all these cooking competitions on your television, 'Ready, Steady Cook,' 'Can't Cook, Won't Cook,' 'Master Chef'—all competitions. Competition is big here in England. Need I go on?"

Brack was quiet for a moment, obviously thinking about my plan, then he reached across the table and took my hand. "I think you've just saved our Sweet Whippo campaign. I vote yes. I have every confidence in you. Develop it as soon as possible."

I was so elated that I squeezed his hand back so hard he winced. I could stay in London.

"How about Will?" I said, pulling back my hand to let a waiter start clearing the dishes. "He may not like the idea. I have this feeling he wants me to trot back to New York as soon as possible, but I definitely do not want to go."

Brack smiled at me, a really satisfied smile. "You leave Will to me," he said, handing me the menu. "You write up the plan as soon as possible and send me a fax in Helsinki, as that's where I'll be for the next few days."

I almost blurted out that Will was coming to the flat this evening. Why didn't I? I tried to cover myself by saying that I would of course explain the ideas to Will and work closely with him. Brack didn't appear to notice my stammering sentences.

I ate my chocolate cannelloni filled with pistachio cream with delight. I could now go on working here in London and I could go on seeing Braxton Clark. Seeing Braxton Clark turned out to be the easy part, as he asked me right then and there if I were free for dinner and a play on Friday when he got back from Finland.

He walked me back to my flat, turned down my offer of coffee but gave me a serious kiss and hug at the door. I could tell that he and I were headed for an intimate relationship, I really could, because all of a sudden I couldn't remember what Danny looked like.

Then Pauline Greene showed up and I was foolish and egotistical enough to let myself get sucked into her whirlpool of lies, accusations, and danger.

Chapter 9

I hardly recognized Pauline when she arrived at my door just fifteen minutes after Brack left. Her cap of straw-colored hair was wet and sticking to her forehead, her eyes were red-rimmed, her cheeks tear-stained and her face blotched and bare of any makeup. She had on the same suit she'd worn at our big meeting this morning, now well wrinkled. I led her in, sat her down on the sofa. I had already brewed a pot of strong tea—four o'clock began the sacred British teatime—and I got that, together with some chocolate cookies, put it on the tray with the cups, sugar bowl and milk pitcher, put it on the table in front of her and told her to drink up. I pulled up a chair and sat down, facing her.

She obeyed, draining her cup quickly and holding it out for another filling.

"Thanks, Lucille," she said. "I've been walking round and round the block here for hours, waiting for you. I can't talk to anyone else, particularly to the people at the office. They wouldn't believe me. But you're new here and don't know about Fiona." She took a gulp of tea and looked around at the flat, her eyes roving from corner to corner, but made no comment. Was she looking for that box of chocolates or maybe for a crumpled-up note?

"What should I know about Fiona?" I asked.

Pauline gave me a calculating look before she answered, obviously not even sure she should trust me. She took a pill from her handbag and swallowed it quickly, defiantly.

"What I mean is, Fiona was right in the middle of something very exciting, something she couldn't tell me about, but it was obviously going to be really big. She gave me a few hints, but she swore me to secrecy so nobody in our office could know."

I waited.

"She rang me on Saturday morning to see how the work on Sweet Whippo was going and told me that things were coming to a head on her big project and she'd rather not come in unless I needed her. Then I rang *her* on Sunday afternoon to tell her everything was fine and she told me she was expecting this man—the man she would work with—to come over that night. She wouldn't tell me his name, but now I realize he has to be the one who killed her."

"Pauline, I'm afraid I don't quite follow you. Why would this mystery man want to kill her?"

"Because Fiona said to me, 'When he finds out about this, he's going to kill me.' She laughed when she said it, but now I believe he really did kill her by throwing her down those stairs. Fiona was so graceful and she would never have tripped and fallen on her own. He pushed her!" Pauline tossed her head, flinging that straw hair out of her face, and fixed me with a triumphant look.

"Pauline, that was just a figure of speech, you know that. She didn't really mean he was actually going to kill her." I found it uncanny that we had the same idea about Fiona being knocked down those stairs, but I wasn't going to let on to her.

"Fiona always means what she says."

Poor Pauline, her worship of Fiona was pushing her over the edge.

"Have you told the police this theory?" I asked, picking my words carefully.

"I told Mr. Hammersmith, because he's the one who's dealing with them, and he said he would tell the detective in charge, but for me not to tell anybody else. But I just had to. I don't think he believed me."

"I thought you said Fiona was going to Paris with Will Hammersmith for the weekend. What was she doing at home?"

"Oh, their plans changed," Pauline said airily, "but she'd left me in charge of Sweet Whippo, since I've always done most of the work."

"So she was here in London all weekend?" I was still thinking about those chocolates.

"Why is that important?" Pauline said. "What I want you to do is to make sure that Mr. Hammersmith has told the police about the man who came to see her. I know there was someone because I went by Fiona's flat on my way here and talked to the woman who lived downstairs. She said a man drove up in a big black Jaguar and went up to Fiona's flat Sunday evening. So there."

"Did this woman see what the man looked like?"

"It was raining lightly and getting dark so she couldn't see too well with just the light over the front door, but said he was tall and had on a raincoat and had a sheet of newspaper over his head as he ran down the pavement to the door."

That description could fit most of the men in London on a rainy night.

Pauline drained her second cup, reached for and ate two cookies before fixing me with a piercing look. She had this triumphant but slightly loony look in her eyes.

"Mr. Hammersmith will listen to *you*. If he doesn't, I want you to go to the police yourself. Will you help me? I found out the name of the man in charge. It's Detective Inspector Johnson Reid. We could go together to see him."

I waited a moment, then said, "Pauline, of course I will talk to Will, but I'm sure he's told the police what you asked him to."

"I don't trust him," she said flatly. "I forgot to tell you that Fiona said *he* had come over in the early evening himself. He's also part of this big new project."

I knew that Will had a Jaguar. Could he have driven back later and attacked poor Fiona? But why would he?

"It probably had something to do with Sweet Whippo," I said.

Pauline shook her head. "I don't think so, because Fiona would have told me about that. We've worked so closely on that product. It's something else, something very secret."

I gave up. Pauline was too much for me. I stood up and said, "Yes, Pauline, I'll talk to Will Hammersmith very soon and remind him. I don't think we should go to the police unless we have a definite identification of the man that woman downstairs saw."

I wanted her out of the flat before Will showed up. Pauline might well think we were in cahoots.

Pauline didn't move. "Oh, and I also need your help with tidying up Fiona's papers," she said. "I talked to her mother in Scotland this afternoon and she said she would appreciate it if I could go to the flat and get all Fiona's important papers and send them to her because she needs the insurance bumph. I don't want anybody else from the office to go with me because they're too nosy about Fiona. Mrs. Gordon will try to come down in a fortnight and clear out the flat. Fiona's body is being shipped to Hawick, that's where they live, for the funeral."

With that Pauline started sniffling again, her head down, her hand pleating and unpleating her skirt. I got up to get her a box of tissues, but I stayed on my feet, hoping to move her from that couch. "Of course, I'll go with you to her flat. Just tell me when."

She controlled her sniffing. "Tomorrow afternoon. I told Mr. Hammersmith I would do it. I have a key, you know. Fiona gave me one long ago. I'll ring you after lunch and we'll leave from the office."

I finally got her up and out the door. She was still thanking me as she disappeared down the hall toward the lifts. I watched until she was safely in one before I went back into the flat. I didn't know what to think or even whether to believe Pauline. It wasn't much to go on. A downstairs neighbor seeing a man in a raincoat protecting his head from the rain with a newspaper going into the building was all we had. Pauline had said that Will had been there earlier in the evening and the neighbor downstairs had probably seen his car. Weren't they supposed to be in the midst of an affair? No, to my way of thinking, their getting together on this so-called new project was just one more way for them to find something to mess up my role in the Sweet Whippo campaign. Pauline was just being dramatic. Yet, something made me believe her.

I barely had time to change into a pair of comfortable black cotton slacks and a pink linen shirt, clear off the tea tray, put the cups in the sink and get out the ice before Will was announced by the doorman, five minutes early. I noticed Pauline had eaten all the cookies. Poor girl probably hadn't eaten anything since this disastrous morning. Idly, I wondered what happened to all that food she and her staff were busy preparing before the bad news hit. Was it still waiting in that super kitchen? No, Pauline and the staff would have put it all away neatly.

When I let him in, Will looked me over as carefully as he always did. He nodded his head, approving of my outfit, I guessed.

"How about a drink?" I asked, moving over to the drinks table. "I need one. Pauline was just here."

"Pauline! Why was she here?" he demanded.

"She wanted comforting. Fiona was her idol," I said, as I turned and handed him a glass. "Fix your own and there's ice if you use it."

He poured himself a large whiskey, ignored the ice, added a splash of soda from the siphon bottle and stood there, still watching me.

I thought I would get it over with, even shock him, so I said, "Pauline said she told you that Fiona was expecting a visitor that night and she thinks it was that man who threw Fiona down the stairs and killed her."

Will, calm as ever, said. "Yes, she did, but I didn't believe the poor cow. I told her not to spread that story all over town. She's not quite right in the head, I'm afraid."

"She said you promised to tell the police that. Did you?"

"Of course I mentioned it, but they dismissed it. They have no reason to think Fiona's death was anything but an accident. Those are wicked stairs."

"Been there often?" I asked, innocently.

"Enough." He wasn't giving anything away.

"Pauline said Fiona also told her you visited in the early evening."

He turned on me, frowning, his eyes narrowed. "Pauline talks too much. Of course I was there that evening because

Fiona and I were going over the Sweet Whippo presentation for Monday morning."

I didn't contradict him as I figured they had indeed been busy working on their master plan to dump me.

He took a swig of his drink and walked over to the mantelpiece. Why is it men always do this, leaning casually against it, drink in hand? Even if there's no fire in the fireplace?

"It's because of Fiona's death that we must talk," he began. "I've been talking to Braxton Clark and we both agreed that we'd better scuttle the campaign. Fiona was such an important part of it that we feel it might be a little callous to go on. She was a vital person in the food establishment, you know."

"When did you have this talk with Braxton Clark?"

"Oh, this morning after the meeting and after we talked to the police. I'm very sorry about this, but you can see that your role in the campaign is no longer necessary and so you don't have to stay around these last weeks. I'm sure you'll be glad to get home." He smiled, Cheshire Cat style. Smug.

I smiled back; in fact, I grinned widely. "Then I have news for you. I had lunch with Mr. Braxton Clark and *we* made a decision together. The campaign goes on. Do you want to hear the new proposal?"

I really thought he would lose it. His face paled as he slammed the glass down on the mantel and walked toward me. "You had lunch with Clark?" I backed away.

"Yes, indeed. We had a long, productive lunch and he's agreed to the new proposal. He said he would talk to you about it soon." I tried to keep the triumph out of my voice.

"Got him sewed up, have you?" Will said.

"Got the campaign sewed up," I replied. "I think it's a good idea and if you will just listen, I think you'll agree that it sidesteps the problem of Fiona's death neatly."

He walked back to the fireplace, stood there with his back to me briefly, then picked up his drink, turned and walked over to the sofa, sat down, crossed his beautifully tailored pants legs neatly and gazed at his polished shoes. He was back in control of his emotions when he looked up and said, "I'm all ears."

So I gave him a brief outline of my ideas. It had to be brief as I hadn't had a chance to really work through all the ramifications. His face didn't show any reaction even though he listened closely. When I finished, he was quiet for a moment, then sighed and got up from the sofa.

"I don't know what to say to you. You're obviously going your own way regardless. I just hope you know what you are doing." He took a last swallow of his drink, looked down into the bottom of the glass and then added, "I still think we'd be better off canceling or at least postponing the introduction, but since you have this 'in' with the client"— and now there was a slight sneer in his voice—"we'll have to go along with it. Best of British luck to you."

He walked over to the door, turned, said, "Thanks for the drink," and was gone. I couldn't believe that he had given up so easily. Something was going on that I simply could not fathom.

Was he heading straight for a telephone or visit to Brack to reconvince him to—as he put it—"scuttle" the campaign? It was obvious to me that I had better get right to work to get my brilliant plan moving. There was no way I was going to leave London and Brack without a fight.

One more thing. I decided I would accept Pauline's theory about Fiona's death, partly because it was also mine, but also because I knew she would not give up lightly. Pauline might be slightly loony, but she also might be right.

Wouldn't it be a slap in the face to London Office if Lucille Anderson, New York Office émigré, solved this case and was congratulated by Scotland Yard? Then again, I had a sobering thought. Whoever was sending me nasty notes and chocolates and possibly stalking me would obviously prefer to see the ashes of Lucille Anderson, neatly packaged and labeled, sent back to New York Office by UPS.

Put up or shut up, Lucille. I decided I would take my chances.

Chapter 10

After Will left, I staggered along to the bedroom and flopped down on the bed. I might be smug about my victory over Will and his plans to send me back to New York, but I was also exhausted and confused after this wild day. Was Pauline really off her head or was she telling the truth? What game was Will playing? And Lucille, how are you going to pull off this crazy idea about a chefs' Sweet Whippo cook-off? Have you bitten off much, much more than you can chew?

I wanted to mix myself another tall drink and just lie there watching television, but I forced myself to get up and go out to the drawing room, look in my briefcase for Jane's telephone number and phone her. She was home, but before I could say anything, she started immediately asking about my health.

"I hope you went straight home and to bed," she said. "Everyone was so worried about you. I was."

"Jane, you won't believe what has happened," I said quickly, breaking into her solicitousness. I told her about the lunch with Brack and my idea of the Sweet Whippo chefs' cook-off. She was obviously stunned and kept making gulping noises, but eventually rallied round and even expressed guarded enthusiasm.

"Jane, we've got to get together early tomorrow morning

and work on this new campaign. First, though, please get a few names of some great British chefs so we can pick one. I'll be responsible for getting the American one. Yes, yes I know, it's short notice, but I want to get this plan faxed to Clark in Helsinki before Will figures out a way to delay it."

I told her then how Will had shown up to tell me the campaign was off and that he had not taken graciously to the new plan and right now was probably bending the ear of the head of London Office, imploring him to send me back to New York.

I left her muttering and sputtering but ready to help. Then, exhausted or not, I got on the telephone to America, taking advantage of the time difference to make a necessary telephone call. My long-time friend Alex at the Culinary Institute of America (known familiarly as the other CIA) at Hyde Park, New York, was in her office and I told her my plan. She liked it and promised to come through with at least four names of chef graduates who would respond well to this kind of challenge. Then I got on to my laptop and banged out a plan. This plan wasn't completely off the wall, as I had done something similar a few years ago with a bunch of U.S. chefs competing against each other with recipes for a product we were then pushing. Of course that was real food—a new flavor of a pudding—not this weird Sweet Whippo stuff.

I finished by midnight and fell into bed. Did I fall asleep right away? Of course not, because all I could think about was Pauline and her theory of Fiona being thrown down the steps. No matter what I had told Pauline, and no matter that Will Hammersmith thought Pauline was nuts, I believed her. Tomorrow I would certainly go with her to Fiona's flat and I would do my best to nose around to see what I could find out about Fiona and her "special project."

Would this be my first real case of detective work in London? Why not? What did I have to lose?

Did I imagine it or did the people in the offices of the Public Relations Department view me with polite but incredulous looks as I strode through to my office? Jane must have got in early and spread the news around about the new campaign. I printed out my proposal, scribbled notes on it and handed it to Kathy, our super-secretary, to turn it out in her usual perfect British syntax and grammar. She had already been kind enough to point out to me last week some of the American spelling she'd had to correct, not to mention a few minor gaffes in some of my earlier efforts.

"I wouldn't use the expression, 'On-the-Job Training,' " she had said gently. "Over here, 'On the Job' can mean sex."

I had laughed and thanked her for her editing and told her we Americans had a lot to learn about these subtle differences.

Today, she got the correct fax number from Brack's office, then sent the program off to him in Helsinki, along with a covering note from me. I also gave a copy to Jane to study. Pauline called me later in the morning to say she was leaving for Fiona's flat after a quick lunch and would stop by to pick me up. I explained the situation to Jane, who expressed much interest in seeing what Fiona's flat looked like and offered to go along. I told her Pauline wouldn't approve, but I promised to tell her in great detail about the furnishings. When Pauline walked into my office, I was relieved to see that she looked calm, with her hair carefully combed, and wearing a lightweight woolen suit in a pale shade of gray set off by a light blue shirt. At least she wasn't wearing funereal black.

"How are you today, Pauline?"

"Fine," she snapped. "At least as fine as one can be when one's best friend dies."

I dreaded the hour ahead.

We took a taxi to Fiona's flat in Chelsea. The building must have been a former townhouse and was very narrow with five stories, the front door painted a bright red. Pauline took out her keys and opened the door. Inside there was a door to the right, which I assumed was to the flat where that downstairs neighbor resided. I looked up at those polished grayish-white marble stairs and tried to put the image of Fiona out of my mind, the picture of her tumbling down these same stairs. They were steep and they were hard.

We walked up them carefully without a word to each other; then Pauline put another key into the door of the flat and stepped aside politely to let me in. There was a small foyer with a highly polished side table and mirror which reflected a coat stand in the corner. A door from this room led into a carpeted drawing room furnished with a sofa covered in a peach-colored silky fabric facing a coffee table. A chair upholstered in the same fabric was at one end of the coffee table. Against the wall was a secretary desk with a glass-fronted cabinet above filled with books. There were small tables with lamps and vases scattered around the room, one vase still holding some very wilted freesias. The room looked like Fiona—smart and glossy.

Pauline walked straight through this room to another door, opened it and beckoned me into a room with long windows overlooking a garden. This Fiona had turned into a combined dining area and kitchen. There were elegant Smallbone cabinets and appliances discreetly built in. Shiny copper pots hung from a rack above a work island. No expense had been spared. I bet myself that she had got it all as a freebie because of her influence in the food world.

"She did a lot of her recipe development here," Pauline offered. "Gave wonderful little dinner parties." She shook her head sadly. I murmured appropriate appreciation.

From there we went into a bedroom which looked like something out of the British edition of *House Beautiful*—all restrained glamour. A double bed took up the center of the room, flanked by a nightstand on either side. A dressing table faced the opaque curtains at the windows. There was a wardrobe and a chest next to a half-open louvered door, showing a capacious closet. I knew the adjoining bathroom would be perfect, and it was. Plenty of mirrors and marble with crystal jars of bath gels and soaps lining the counters. The smell was expensive—more freesia and roses. Aside from a pair of tights draped to dry over a towel rod, there was no evidence of Fiona's last hours here. The place was too tidy. Had someone been in here to clean up or after Fiona's fall? Had the police taken fingerprints in the flat? I didn't think so, because there was no evidence of powder dust. Or did police still do fingerprints that way? I must find out because of my own novel. If ever I got back to work on it.

Pauline sighed again as she walked back to the drawing room and I followed.

"Her mother asked me to get any insurance policies, papers, things like that, as soon as possible. I'm sure they're in the desk." She moved a chair over, pulled down the desk flap and started removing papers from the pigeonholes. "The police looked around the flat when they were here, but didn't remove anything, Mr. Hammersmith said. I'm going up to Scotland in a fortnight for the funeral, just a family one. Mr. Hammersmith also said there will be a me-

morial service here in London and Fiona's mother will
come down for that." She dropped the papers on the desk
flap and put her head in her hands.

"What do you want me to do now?" I asked her as I
stood there awkwardly. I hoped she wasn't going to weep.

Pauline took a deep breath and looked up. "Maybe you
could start with the dressing table in the bedroom and
check for any papers, and then those tables by her bed.
Fiona always did a lot of her work in bed."

I'll say, was the nasty thought that crossed my mind,
then felt ashamed. The poor woman was dead.

I didn't really want to look through any private papers of
Fiona's. It seemed an invasion. I hoped she wasn't a saver
of love letters. I certainly was not, although I had to admit I
had received very few letters in the past years to save.
Danny was not the writing type.

In the bedroom, I sat down first at the dressing table and
pulled out the shallow center drawer, then the side ones. All
were full of jars and bottles, some samples of various mois-
turizers, creams, colognes, perfumes. Looked like Fiona
was a thrifty type and never threw anything away.

No papers at all in the dressing table I could report to
Pauline. The chest was crammed with silken underwear and
hosiery, but there were no papers, no little boxes of carefully saved letters. Next I went over to the bedside tables. If
she were anything like me, this would be where she stuffed
in memos, half-written reports, ruled pads with words scribbled, maybe a diary. I was right, because the drawers of one
table contained a crossword puzzle book with most of the
squares neatly filled in, in ink. Silently I applauded her. I
had yet to master the British crossword puzzle with its ana-
grams and quotations—even though I did the Sunday *New
York Times* puzzle with a pen—and here she had finished al-

most an entire collection of the *Sunday Telegraph* ones.

A drawer in the other table yielded a writing portfolio, a soft leather cover enclosing a pad of white ruled paper. On the left side a few folded pages of neat writing were held in the pocket and on the right a page was half filled. I was nosy enough to read this, at first quickly scanning it and then slowing down when I saw the words, "Sweet Whippo versus S&C" on the page. What was "S&C"? I sat down on the bed, took out the folded pages from the pocket and spread them out on the bed. One page was a draft of a letter, with no name or address at the top. But the words on the page intrigued me.

Pauline's voice from the drawing room startled me. "I'm almost finished here," she said. "What about you?"

"Same here," I said, reading faster. Fiona's writing, each 't' crossed and 'i' dotted in this rough draft of a letter, together with some scratched-out sentences, seemed to be about a plan which involved a campaign for a rival product, something identified as "S&C."

I heard Pauline coming in my direction. I don't know what made me do it—yes, I do, it was this wicked detective streak in me—but I folded the sheets back up, tore off the half-finished page from the folder, and stuffed them all into my handbag. I told myself that it was because I really should know Fiona's ideas for Sweet Whippo as part of our overall plan. I left the writing portfolio and the crossword puzzles displayed on the bed. Pauline entered the room, carrying a large brown filing envelope tied with a ribbon tucked under one arm.

"Unless Fiona had a safe deposit box, this is all I could find. Her will is here and some insurance papers," she said.

I pointed to the bed. "There's what I found in the bed-side tables and there were no papers in the dressing table or chest. Did she keep a diary?" Only half a lie.

Pauline looked sharply at me, but said, "I don't really know. You didn't find one?"

I didn't have to lie about that and just shook my head. She put the big envelope on the bed and opened the writing portfolio, looked inside quickly, dropped it back onto the bed and picked up the book of completed crossword puzzles.

"She could work these like lightning. Ever so quick."

"Ever so, our Fiona," I agreed.

Pauline walked over to the door to the closet and opened it, almost with a flourish. Fiona's closet was so neat that I actually gaped at it. Clothes were hung on satin hangers, shoes neatly lined up below, sweaters and blouses stacked on shelves. Pauline reached in and pulled out a hanger with a shimmery long dress on it. She gazed at it and I thought for one wild moment she was going to bury her face in it, but she sighed and put it back. She looked briefly at the tidy lineup and then closed the door.

"No place for papers here. I just can't get it into my head that Fiona is actually gone, never coming back. She loved clothes."

And lethal shoes, I said to myself.

"Is there any other place where she would keep necessary papers, you know, or any of her work here in the flat?" I asked. I wanted to know more about S&C, to be brutally frank.

"I shouldn't think so," Pauline said. "I will ask her bank if she had a safe deposit box. I guess we should go back to the office now." She put the book of puzzles and the leather portfolio back into the night table drawer. She picked up the large envelope on the bed, stared at the bed itself for a brief moment, then turned and walked slowly toward the flat's front door. I followed.

The papers were burning a hole in my conscience and I wanted to get out of that flat fast, go somewhere private where I could reread Fiona's writing. I kept telling myself it was my duty to find out everything because of loyalty to our campaign and to MWVB.

Pauline closed and locked the door to the flat and we walked slowly and carefully down the steps. It was even easier now to see how Fiona could have gone down them, especially if she tripped over a flared leg of her pants on the landing at the top. I was surprised that Pauline hadn't gone off on another speech about Fiona being killed on these stairs, but she seemed unusually calm. Then she startled me by knocking on the door of the ground-floor flat on our way out.

"I want you to talk to this woman," she said. "She's the one who saw the car."

No, Pauline hadn't given up her mission.

We waited a few moments and Pauline knocked again. The door was finally opened by a woman who looked to be around fifty or so, her gray hair perfectly coiffed and her tall, thin figure clothed in a dark green two-piece knitted suit. She looked us over, not smiling.

"You remember me, Mrs. Tate," Pauline said, hurriedly. "I talked to you yesterday about my friend Fiona Gordon who lived upstairs and who was killed when she fell down these stairs."

The woman nodded, looking me over carefully.

"This is my friend from the office who was helping me collect the insurance papers from her flat," Pauline went on. "I want you to tell her what you saw, I mean, about the car."

"Why?" the woman asked.

Pauline seemed taken aback.

"Well, because I don't want people to think I'm making it all up."

"I told the police the same thing I told you," said the woman. "That's the end of the case, isn't it? They said it was an accident. I really don't want to get involved any further."

Pauline was adamant. "Would you tell my friend here what you told me? Please."

The woman sighed. "I merely told them that in the late evening I saw a dark green or black car parked in front and a man get out, run up the pavement to our door. I heard him come in and go up the stairs. I assumed it was a friend of Miss Gordon's. I couldn't actually see what the man looked like because he had on a raincoat and had this newspaper over his head. It was raining."

I opened my mouth to see if I could get more information but she smiled a wintry smile and closed the door, politely but firmly, in our faces.

I turned to look at Pauline, who had a smug look on her face as she said, "See? I told you someone was here, someone who could have killed her."

I shook my head. "That description covers too many people, and how do you know it wasn't Will Hammersmith, who was here earlier, like you said?"

"Will could never have killed Fiona," Pauline said. "He was insanely jealous of her, you know. But I now think it was Braxton Clark! Do you want to know why? Let's get back to the office and I'll tell you why!"

Chapter 11

Too stunned to say anything, I followed Pauline meekly as she strode out to the sidewalk, hailed a taxi and climbed in, beckoning me to join her.

"What did you mean, you suspect Braxton Clark?" I demanded after she had told the driver our destination. "Tell me."

"I figured it out just now," she replied, still sounding smug. "He and Fiona were practically engaged last year, and then she started seeing Mr. Hammersmith. Braxton Clark was livid, Fiona told me. You heard what Mrs. Tate said, and Mr. Clark is tall, and Fiona used to talk about riding around in his big Jaguar. I am going to tell Mr. Hammersmith as soon as we get back to the office and he can tell the police."

Was that all she had to base her belief on? I was weak with relief.

"Pauline, I think you have to have more evidence than what Mrs. Tate says," I said firmly. "I think you are making a mistake going to Will Hammersmith with gossip."

Pauline folded her arms and sat there, lower lip stuck out in defiance. "I do have more evidence, but I am not going to tell you. You wouldn't understand," she said.

"What evidence?" I persisted.

"You'll find out."

I gave up and sat back on the cab seat, trying to work out how I was going to handle this situation. She was silent, lost in her own thoughts, ignoring my sidelong glances at her. When we got back to the offices, she jumped out, insisted on paying the cab driver and disappeared with just a wave of the hand. Off to see Will, I'll bet. Would he believe her accusations of Brack or would he brush her off?

I walked to my office quickly, asked Kathy to send out for a sandwich and opened my bag to get out those purloined papers. I spread them out on my desktop, but before I could start reading them, Jane knocked and came in to report on her activities. I quickly put them out of sight in the center drawer. She had put so many wheels in motion that I could hardly keep up with her. Together we went over her lists and I was so immersed in work that I had no time to look at the papers.

I had been too chicken to tell Pauline about the new Whippo Cook-off plan when we were in Fiona's flat, giving myself the excuse that the plan was still not approved. But Jane had already turned up the names of three celebrated British chefs, and now Pauline had to know that the campaign would go on without Fiona and that the test kitchen would be involved only in working with the chefs.

I couldn't face Pauline again so I asked Jane to go down to the kitchen to explain to Pauline and her staff about the plan and to say that we were also doing this as a tribute to Fiona. I ate my sandwich and talked on the telephone with Barry in New York to tell him about the new campaign. He was surprised but pleased to hear how I had come up with this idea.

"Your session over there has turned dramatic," he said dryly. "We heard about that woman's death."

"I guess Will Hammersmith has talked to you about sending me back."

There was a silence and then a short laugh. "He obviously didn't know you well enough, Lucille. I'm glad you're hanging in there. Don't let the Brits push you around. We need your success, you know. Things are even more tense around here." He didn't elaborate, just asked me to tell him more about my new campaign.

We talked on while I bounced some ideas off him. His confidence in me was all I needed, and when I hung up, I felt ready to cope again. I even called Danny and had a brief but reassuring conversation about how important I was to him.

"Don't get mixed up in anything about this woman's death, Lucy," he said. "I know how fascinated you are with death and mystery, but I don't want you in any trouble. I wish you would come back here, and soon."

I hoped I hadn't let on how much I wanted to stay in London, with this new man, Brack. I felt a little guilty.

Jane reported back that her little speech went surprisingly well, with most of the kitchen staff, nodding and murmuring approval, even though Pauline looked balky. I showed Jane the list that Alex at the Culinary Institute had faxed this morning and I spent the rest of the day on the telephone, in fact well into early evening, trying to get through to each of them. Chefs are notoriously hard to pull away from their kitchens to come to a telephone, but I finally talked to three. It was hard to explain exactly what Sweet Whippo was—or wasn't—to the chefs.

"It's not just a whipped cream substitute, it's not a total sugar substitute, it's not exactly a total fat substitute, and it has no salt, no cholesterol but plenty of fiber. It's sort of a combination product that can be worked into many foods." This usually led to a prolonged silence while the chef balanced his reputation against thoughts about money and publicity.

"It's not dangerous to your health, I am assured," I kept on. "It's a new wave product, the first of its kind over here," I added. I usually received noncommittal grunts at this stage. But I persisted and the one chef that seemed eager to tackle the cook-off was one I knew slightly. Bobby Johnson—or Chef Robert, as he preferred to be known now, French pronunciation of that last "t," please. He had been featured in a public relations program for another New York Office client and had done a good job. He had just left one restaurant where he'd been executive chef and wanted time out before he took on another job and he also wanted to see what the best chefs were doing in London. I bribed him with tales of new restaurants here, all expenses paid, television appearances, etc. I had decided against a classic pastry chef for fear I would end up with candied flowers and carved swans and decided instead to see if an American chef could present Sweet Whippo in interesting but simple desserts and main dish foods. I had really wanted to choose a woman for this job but knew it would be politically awkward to substitute a woman chef for Fiona.

Picking the right British chef was a little trickier, but Jane proved good at that. She approached two of them by telephone and, in between conversations, came in to report her progress. We talked about these men and she said that Pauline knew them and approved. In between conversations, I couldn't seem to keep my mind off Pauline and her determination to prove that Fiona was murdered and by Brack. I decided to pump Jane.

"Did Pauline say anything about Fiona being murdered when you talked to her about these chefs?" I said as casually as possible as I looked down at Jane's comprehensive notes.

When I looked up, Jane was staring at me. "No. She never said a word about Fiona's death. Why, does Pauline really think Fiona was murdered?"

"She seems obsessed by it. I don't know what to think. Did Fiona have any enemies?"

Jane shrugged. "She was known for playing both ends against the middle, never missing a chance to get what she wanted. I guess I shouldn't talk about her like that now that she's dead," she said apologetically, "but I was always a little afraid of her. Maybe she knifed one too many persons and somebody got back at her." Jane seemed to be warming to this conversation. "She had a string of lovers, you know, and I'll bet one of them got jealous and tossed her down those stairs," she added. "What exactly is Pauline saying? She was very close to our Fiona. Worshiped her. I'll bet she knows who could have done the deed."

"Jane," I said hastily, "you're too bloodthirsty." I wasn't about to repeat Pauline's accusations of our client, Braxton. That would go all over the office like wildfire. I was already worried enough that Pauline had talked to the other girls in the kitchen about her suspicions.

I remembered those papers of Fiona's in my desk drawer and ached to get them out and read them. But Jane had already gone back to work and was discussing the merits of each of the British chefs on that list.

Our conversation was cut short by the ring of the telephone. It was Brack in Helsinki, talking about the campaign, giving me total approval and telling me he'd be back tomorrow night and to save the evening for him.

"Bully for us," I said as I put down the telephone. "Braxton Clark has approved our plan. I'm seeing him tomorrow evening to go over the fine points."

Jane raised one eyebrow then grinned and gave me the thumbs up sign. "Let me know the details," she said. "All the details."

When Jane finally left my office, I pulled out Fiona's scribblings on the sheets of papers. I puzzled over them again. They certainly seemed to be rough drafts of a letter plus an outline of a publicity plan for this product named S&C. The plan seemed suspiciously like Fiona's original ideas for Sweet Whippo, as she had suggestions for recipes for dessert dishes. The letter had no address or even heading and just had one paragraph about an enclosed plan. Had she actually rewritten and sent this material to somebody? I read the words again and decided Fiona was indeed proposing a plan for a rival product to Sweet Whippo, as our product was mentioned several times. Crafty old Fiona, it looked like to me, was pitching for a new job somewhere with somebody. But who? And why? I'd have to ask Brack if there was another product similar to Sweet Whippo out there somewhere. Another totally synthetic product, perhaps. It was a horrible thought that maybe our future would be a cuisine of synthetic products taking the place of good old grown-in-dirt food.

I folded up the papers and put them into my bag to take home. They shouldn't be left lying around in this office. When I got home, I puzzled over them again for a long time, then put them aside. I really didn't have the time or energy to think about what to do next. So much for my first detective case. I didn't seem to be furthering my literary career here either, as my manuscript lay untouched. I hadn't counted on such a heavy schedule in London Office.

★ ★ ★ ★ ★

The next day was filled with so much work that I actually forgot about Fiona and her plan. There was absolute silence—not even any memos—from Will, but I figured he was sulking. I wanted to beard Pauline again and see if I could get some sense out of her about why she suspected Brack, but she had disappeared and her assistant said she was attending to some of Fiona's possessions. I figured Pauline *was* off her rocker with her accusations about Brack and it was up to me to find out the truth and then confront her.

When Brack showed up at the flat, he seemed genuinely pleased to see me and we walked to another restaurant nearby, where I promised that I would not batter his ears telling him about all the work Jane and I had until after we'd eaten. As a matter of fact, I never got around to telling him anything about our work because we spent our time talking, talking, talking to each other about life and what we wanted from it. We strolled back to the flat to have coffee and finish our talk and we ended up in that nice big bed. You never know about these Englishmen.

I told myself that a good sex life would improve my productivity and work. I didn't want to admit to myself that I was hopelessly gone on the man and was afraid if I played too hard to get, there might not be enough time left to see what might develop before I had to go back to New York City—and Danny.

Brack and I agreed that we would be discreet about this situation, saying that our colleagues would be better off not realizing that some of the best campaign ideas might possibly be agreed on through pillow talk. It was not that we were unromantic, far from it, but you can spend only so much time in loving embraces and recuperative sleep. I could see some busy days and nights ahead.

I admit that when I woke up in the early hours of the morning and looked over at his face, Pauline's words suddenly came back to me and I felt a chill. But how could anyone as great as Brack want to kill someone like Fiona? No, Pauline was obviously grasping at straws. I would find out and prove to her that he was nowhere near Fiona's flat that fateful night.

Chapter 12

The rest of the week flew by. Although every morning I approached my office with trepidation, fearing to see another of those nasty notes, I was spared. Both Jane and I were busy with meetings needed to let the advertising side know about the new chefs. I had some problems with a few account reps, but I made it plain that I would not back down, so they could just wait until our public relations program was firm. Jane and I wrote down ideas and copy slants and photo suggestions until we were exhausted. I called Barry again to tell him what was being accomplished, and I knew he was pleased that I had taken over the situation in a truly New York Office manner. I didn't tell him about the nasty notes or the chocolates and I certainly didn't tell him about sleeping with the client. Barry could be a bit puritan at times. Those chocolates were still in my freezer, because I wasn't quite sure where to go to get them analyzed.

When I finally heard from Will, he offered no more delaying tactics. I figured Braxton had had a quiet word with him. He was definitely chilly on the telephone.

"Did Pauline tell you her newest idea about Fiona's death? She says Braxton Clark murdered her." I laughed lightly, but it came out slightly choked.

Will said, "Silly cow. I told her to say no more about murder and to keep her gawp shut and stop these ridiculous accusations. I talked to the police just this morning and they told me they definitely were not pursuing the case and were accepting it as accidental death."

I knew that Pauline would not agree. I tried to quiz Will about why Pauline would accuse Braxton Clark but he wouldn't bite. He simply hung up.

Finally, it was the weekend and Brack and I could have some time together. He had a spacious, decorator-furnished flat which took up the ground floor of an old house in Enfield, a northern suburb of London, a pretty little village within easy driving distance of his factory. We spent no time at all talking Sweet Whippo, though, and instead got down to the fun of being together—making love, making breakfast, having lunch at this big pub, the Moon Under the Water, a great name, or at the Wonder, a small pub filled with the locals. Then we went for walks in the village in light sunshine, more making love, dinner at a Chinese restaurant, breakfast together eating the sausage, bacon, eggs, tomatoes and toast made by him. "We need a proper English breakfast to keep up our strength," he said, "but I'll spare you the chips, black pudding and baked beans." I appreciated that. I can never understand the Brits' love of beans for breakfast. So we went on making love, reading the *Sunday Times*, the *Telegraph*, even the *Guardian*. Brack was loving, very loving, yet we didn't talk much about anything in our future. I told myself it was his British way and there were still at least four weeks before I had to go back to New York. The weather was perfect June weather, mild and sunny. He told me how good I looked in my lightweight gray woolen slacks (the weather wasn't *that* mild) and a gray-and-white striped shirt with a white cashmere sweater casually knotted around my shoulders. He looked totally different from his client persona by wearing a pair of dark slacks, Leander pink shirt and dark blue sweater. I knew it was Leander pink because he told me so and promised to show me the Leander Club at Henley. We didn't bother with pajamas and nightgowns in bed.

"It's been fantastic, but it's back to Sweet Whippo tomorrow," I said sadly, as we gathered up the scattered newspapers from the floor and sofa on Sunday afternoon and stacked them up neatly. "I'm counting on Pauline to help us because Fiona has trained her so well. Poor Fiona. I admit I am still too curious about her death. But I guess we'll never know what really happened. Even Will says so. He says the police say they have no real proof that it was anything but an accident, so they have closed the case. Death by misadventure or some such Victorian phrase."

I watched him closely for his reaction. We had barely mentioned Fiona during the two days together, but I couldn't get Pauline's accusation of Brack out of my mind. I kept wanting to mention it, but I was afraid any questioning would spoil this wonderful interlude. When I was away from Pauline, I found it hard to believe any of her words.

"What else did Will say?"

"Nothing much. He said the police knew she had a number of friends but they haven't learned who visited her that night, if indeed the woman downstairs was right about a late visitor. Did you know many of her friends?"

Brack didn't answer for a moment. Then he shrugged. "A few. Fiona was a popular woman; she had many, many friends, both men and women, a fair amount in the food field: editors, writers, critics, you know. Fiona probably said goodnight to a friend, saw said friend out the front door, started back upstairs and then tripped and fell." He shook his head sadly. "Those marble steps were beautiful but dangerous. Seems strange the friend hasn't come forward, though. May not have realized he was the last person to see Fiona."

"The lady downstairs claims the visitor was a man and drove a Jaguar. Pauline says she has even more proof that Fiona was killed." I bit my tongue to keep from adding, "By you."

He put down the neat pile of papers with a loud thump on the coffee table. "Is this Pauline the expert on murder? Does she know that I have a Jaguar? Will has one, too. And I imagine a few more of her friends drive around in them. Are we all under suspicion?" He turned to look directly at me. "Why are you so interested?"

"Didn't I ever tell you that I am a mystery nut? Especially British mysteries. Can't get enough of them, either written or on television. It's always been my secret desire to quit public relations and write mysteries and I am actually trying to write one. And here I have a mystery right on my doorstep."

He didn't even smile, but instead said, "I'd really rather you put this particular mystery out of your mind. You've got a lot on your plate just getting this chef contest thing going. Now, I've got to get you back to your flat so I can get organized for a trip to the Continent tomorrow morning."

"Where are you going? How long will you be gone?" God, I sounded like a wife. "I mean, just in case I need to clear anything with you."

He didn't answer for a moment, then said, "Most of the week. I'll ring you one night." He turned away to pick up the stack of newspapers and carry them to the kitchen. "My daily will have these collected tomorrow. Now let's get you back to that flat."

The weekend was ending too quickly for me, but one

thing became perfectly clear. I knew now that Danny was not right for me because I had acquired a taste—literally— for Englishmen. Another thing was not perfectly clear. Brack seemed upset about my going on about Fiona's murder. Was I risking my relationship with him if I kept on being the nosy detective? I had thought several times during the weekend to bring up the subject of those papers from Fiona's bedside table, but something held me back. One thing that kept me from asking him if he knew about "S&C" was that I would have to admit I had learned about it from the stolen papers. My move, which had seemed too clever at the time, was coming back to haunt me, and now I saw myself not as the smart detective but the nosy American. No, I'd wait until some other time, or maybe never. After all, right now what was important was that Brack and I were together. I decided I would put all thoughts of Fiona's possible murder out of my mind until I got this media introduction over with. Forget your ambition to become a detective, let that manuscript wait, Lucille, and concentrate on becoming a successful public relations executive in this alien land or you might not only mess up your job, but also your love life. Yes, I was besotted. Midlife crisis maybe?

On Monday, I called Jane in and said, "These next two weeks with the chefs are going to test us mightily. Bobby Johnson, who insists that he is now Chef Robert, will be here tomorrow and the British one the day after. We've got to interview them and start them working. So we'd better start producing fast."

I wasn't looking forward to asking Pauline's help with our chefs, but she surprised me.

"I'd like to help out in any way," she announced, when I

walked into the test kitchen on Monday morning. "I've given some thought to your idea and I think it may work very well. I think of it now as a fitting memorial to Fiona."

I nodded solemnly.

Pauline's impassive face softened. Today she was garbed in a spotless white uniform-style dress, covered by a bib apron of dark blue. Caro, the Japanese woman on her staff, stood by, nodding at her words. Pauline gave her a tray of dishes and asked her to take them up to somebody called Mr. Palmer, who was waiting to taste them. Then Pauline turned back to me.

"Fiona hired me straight out of my Cordon Bleu cookery course and that was five years ago. We've worked together closely since then, except for the writing. I couldn't begin to write the way she could, all those articles."

Her face crumpled slightly and she turned away, shoving a tray with some small pans on it against a pot on the counter. The noise seemed to startle her.

I braced myself and asked quietly why she thought Braxton Clark had been Fiona's last visitor—and murderer—but she pretended not to hear me and busied herself again with the tray, then moved to the cupboards and took out a vinegar bottle. She turned around and seemed surprised that I was still there.

"I'm working on recipe development for the Finer Margarine account. They told me they would be quite happy for me to do the work and I'm running way behind. If you'll excuse me, please." I left without further conversation. She wasn't going to confide in me. I'd have to tackle her again.

Chef Robert had checked into his small hotel after the overnight flight from JFK and was waiting for us when Jane and I showed up there to take him to lunch where we'd brief him.

"I've already been by the hotel kitchen to say hello to the chef," he said, no jet lag dulling those bright blue eyes. "It's small but well equipped. He's Irish, studied at a culinary school there. Knows his stuff."

I agreed. "The chefs here all know their stuff now, so forget the idea that a lot of people have that English food is not great. That's all changed. You're going to go up against one of the best in this contest. Here's all the information on Sweet Whippo, and we're here to answer any questions. To begin with, let's go to the Connaught Grill. That will give you a good introduction to really good food in London."

Bobby was dressed in a well-tailored dark suit, blue striped shirt and bright red tie, looking more like a Wall Street executive than a hard-working chef, even with his stocky body. I hoped he hadn't forgotten all his fine training at the Culinary Institute.

"Do we have to call you Robert now?" I asked. "I don't want to give it the French pronunciation. You're supposed to be our true-blue American chef."

"Call me Robert, please, with a 't.' I think it sounds better than Bobby; makes me seem older and wiser."

Jane groaned softly. I hoped I hadn't made a big mistake with this chef.

A couple of hours later, all three of us in a better humor from the meal and wine—and the Sweet Whippo budget almost two hundred pounds lighter for our simple lunches of pâté, fresh Scottish salmon, salad, their luscious profiteroles and two bottles of wine—we strolled back to the office. Introductions to Pauline and staff went well, and we left Robert there to taste the dreaded product and went to my office to work out some schedules. He was delivered to my office an hour later, still in good spirits.

"You actually tasted something made with Sweet Whippo?" I asked. "It didn't make you sick?"

"Not bad stuff at all," Bobby said. "Pauline had made a couple of desserts, a cake she called a chocolate gateau, and it wasn't half bad. A little too sweet. Don't worry; I can work with this product. Pastry is not my specialty, but I can certainly knock out some desserts, and since you want to show its versatility, I'd like to try it with some vegetable recipes, something like sweet potatoes."

"I don't think the British eat many sweet potatoes," I said.

"They could learn. How about carrots?"

"Good thought."

"I might even use Whippo in some sauces for meat. A sweet and sour barbecue sauce would be interesting, maybe short ribs would be good, or a rich honey sauce for duck. Wonder what it would be like in a whipped cranberry mousse for turkey?" He smiled that chef-with-a-wonderful-recipe-idea smile.

Jane and I looked at each other and sighed with relief. The first hurdle was over and obviously Robert was ready to start right in with Sweet Whippo.

"Can you work in Pauline's kitchen?" I asked. "I know it's not up to your standard, but for recipe development it should do."

"Sure. I've worked in lot worse kitchens, believe me. You tell me how we handle this, who orders the food, who pays, who cleans up and I'll start tomorrow. After all, you said we should be ready for the press party in three weeks. Hey, this should be fun."

Fun. At least we had one enthusiastic chef. Now for his British counterpart.

★ ★ ★ ★ ★

I braced myself to expect a reticent, stuffy English chef, and that's what I got. At the beginning of the interview also attended by Jane and Pauline the next morning, Chef Nigel Newton was polite and distant and the more we talked, the chillier he got. Apparently Pauline knew him and after a long conversation about Fiona—he had worked with her on some of her magazine articles as well as on a product introduction tour—she seemed to accept him as a substitute for her Fiona. When he saw the cartons of Sweet Whippo and actually opened one, I swear he blanched. But he politely tried out Pauline's proffered dessert pieces, pronounced them quite tasty, and asked for time to discuss the product with Pauline and try it out in his kitchen during the next few days.

He was every inch the professional chef even though his tall frame was clothed in a conservatively-cut dark suit, spotless white shirt and striped tie. He had straight black hair, tied in a small pigtail—his only touch of lightness—brown eyes, sharp nose and a firm mouth. When he put on his high, white chef's toque and white coat, he was going to tower over Robert. They would look like Mutt and Jeff. Not exactly the media image I wanted, but it was too late to do anything about it.

Jane and I left Pauline and our British star together, walking slowly back to my office.

"He's no charm boy, that's for sure," I said. "But Pauline does know him. Do we have to stick with him or can we try out a couple more?"

"He's the one several people said was the best, so I'd like to give him a chance. Seems he's a big favorite with the media. Started a restaurant a few years ago, turned it over to the sous chef and now is sort of a celebrity consultant, turning out books every year, too. Has been on television chef shows. Maybe he smiled a lot more then."

"How come he agreed to consider Sweet Whippo?"

"Sweet publicity, what else? We aren't paying these chefs mega pounds—just expenses and a decent stipend for their time—so they can only hope to gain fame and fortune. But as I said, you know most chefs. They love an audience, not to mention seeing themselves on television and their photographs in all the papers and some magazine. That is, if we're lucky with the media. If we're not, I'm seriously considering taking off for Africa, somewhere out of reach of any telephone or fax."

"Don't start packing yet," I said. "I may join you."

The next few days were wall-to-wall work and meetings. Jane and I left the chefs strictly alone, directing any questions from them to Pauline, who seemed to be getting on extremely well with both of them. Our British chef was rallying round and coming up with good ideas for the product; he seemed to be fascinated with combining Sweet Whippo with fish. Fish! Good luck, Chef Nigel.

At a briefing, Will listened to our description of the chefs and their qualifications without comment. He seemed almost pleasant, with his mind far away, as opposed to his usual shark-like attention to my questions.

"What's new on the Fiona case?" I asked him during one long pause.

He shot me a sharp look, then shrugged. "There's no case. Why don't you just let it go? And I'd appreciate it if you would get that woman Pauline off my back. She's a bloody nuisance with her whining about finding dear Fiona's killer. There is no killer. Period."

I backed off.

Jane wondered aloud about Will's bad temper on our walk back to the office.

"They were having quite an affair, I'm told. Maybe they had a fight and he knocked her down the stairs and now he realizes the police are closing in on him."

"Your imagination is running wild, Jane. Too many television programs."

"Wouldn't put it past him. They both have trigger tempers, but I heard Fiona was chummy with a number of people, so it will probably turn out to be an old lover who visited her and doesn't even know she's dead. Or a young one, a very young one. A toy boy. Maybe Fiona had one of them."

She stopped gossiping for a moment, deep in thought. "No, I think it was a discarded lover. Somebody like Braxton Clark. Wouldn't that be one for the tabloids! Oh, I'm sorry, I forgot you and he are close now. Really sorry."

How did she know that? Did everybody in the office know that Brack and I were sleeping together?

I felt that shock again and realized it was time for me to talk to Brack about Pauline's accusations. I started to ask Jane more questions, but she had already turned quickly into her office, closing the door quietly but firmly.

Brack called me on Wednesday night, and I filled him in on the progress with the chefs. He didn't seem to be worried about Chef Nigel, said he would shape up easily, not to worry. We talked about the coming weekend and he said he wanted us to go away together and he would set up some plans when he got back on Friday. He wanted to go to Henley because his company was going to take a hospitality tent for the big Henley Royal Regatta and he wanted to scout out the area.

"A friend of mine has a house on the other side of the bridge, near the weir. I'll show it to you. You'll like it."

Then he had to go and ruin everything with a telephone call an hour after that, to tell me that plans had changed and we would not be going to Henley this weekend.

"In fact, something has come up and I'd like you to try to get this media introduction done ahead of schedule, within a fortnight. In fact, it must be done within that time. Can you do that? Ring my secretary Pat from time to time and she'll keep me informed."

And he hung up. God, he sounded so cold and business-like. What had I done? A fortnight, that's only two weeks. I was stunned.

Chapter 13

I felt betrayed by that telephone call. Just a few sweet words and then bang, the bad news, which meant that we would have to condense three weeks' work into two. Of course I had to do it, but God help me when I tell this to Jane, the chefs and the ad side. I took a deep breath and started with Jane, who promptly went into shock and kept shaking her head. I asked her to tell the chefs while I filled Will in on the change. When she came to, she rallied round, even smiled. Good old Jane. She finally found her voice.

"I was just about to come into your office and tell you that it's the moment of truth. Chef Robert is ready for us to descend into his domain and taste his first efforts for Sweet Whippo's contest. We can break the news to him now."

Jane and I obediently trooped down to the kitchens and sat at the big bare table. Pauline was at the photo studio, Robert told us, with the other women, so he thought it would be a good time for just the three of us to sample his American food ideas. He was beaming as he placed various dishes in front of us. We took a deep breath, picked up forks and spoons and started in. We both liked the sweet potatoes with honey and Sweet Whippo mixed into them, even though sweet potatoes were not great favorites of many British housewives. I thought the sweet-and-sour spareribs just a little too sweet; we applauded his cranberry mousse, which turned out to be a beautiful light red; both of us disliked the avocado dip—it was too oily—and turned thumbs down on the sauce for scallops.

"These scallops in sauce taste strange, not really American," I said. I kept a wary eye on Robert's watchful face—knowing from experience that chefs can sometimes get very violent when you don't appreciate their efforts. "Are these bay scallops or sea scallops?"

"British sea scallops. Big suckers, too. I thought I'd try something with their seafood," Robert said. "But if you don't like it, we can ditch that one." Thank God he wasn't showing any temperament so far. Dressed in his chef's jacket and pants, white kerchief at his neck and wearing his toque, he made an impressive figure. His bright blue eyes were literally sparkling. "Here, try this cheesecake. Whippo is great as a substitute for cream cheese. Whips like the devil."

"Cheesecake!" I said. "Now that's more like it." And it was. He had made a smooth chocolate one that was creamy and wonderful. "Swear to me that you put Sweet Whippo in this," I said. "It's too good to be true."

Jane was wolfing it down, nodding and smiling.

"Your idea to have dishes from appetizer through dessert for tasting at the media launch is working well," Robert said, as he turned to the refrigerator again. "Of course, Sweet Whippo really works best in desserts, I think. But it works okay in sauces and vegetables if I use a little imagination."

"Forget seafood, maybe."

"No, it's a challenge. I'll come up with something," Robert promised us. "I have already tried shrimp in a dip. I'll get it now."

Pauline chose this moment to walk in. When we turned

guilty faces toward her, she scowled. "I had to come back for some supplies. Sorry to inflict my presence on you in this American feeding frenzy."

"Pauline, you know you are an important part of this campaign, but these American dishes have to pass muster with me first. I don't think you know how they *should* taste, just as I don't know proper British cooking." I was polite but firm.

She sat down, face flushed slightly, but seemed mollified. "Here's a shrimp and onion dip," Robert suggested, putting a bowl of it on the table, together with a plate of potato chips. "I substituted Whippo for most of the sour cream."

Jane took a taste and chewed thoughtfully. "Not too bad, and of course our thrust here is low cholesterol Sweet Whippo, unlike the sour cream which is loaded." I liked it and nodded approval. "Would you like to try some, Pauline?" I asked.

"Please hand me a crisp," she said, and it took me a minute to translate the British crisp into American potato chip.

In silence, we solemnly watched Pauline dip and chew, dip and chew. I thought, has my life really been reduced to dips and chips? Finally, she nodded. "I do think there is merit in this recipe," she pronounced. I didn't dare look at Jane or Robert.

Now was the time, so I started in. "I'm glad we're all here, because I have to tell you some bad news. The media intro has been put forward two weeks," I said quickly, needing to get it over with.

Gasps from Robert and Pauline.

"I know, I know, but Braxton Clark rang me this afternoon to tell me this. He was adamant. So, we'll have to try.

I humbly ask your help."

There were mutterings and mumblings, but finally Robert smiled and said, "No problem."

Pauline said, "My staff will be overextended, but if you can give us authority for overtime charges, we'll try."

I thanked them both profusely.

We discussed the need for more main dish ideas and then Jane and I left Robert happily bashing the dishes and plates around, explaining his recipes to Pauline. Jane went back to her office to contact Chef Nigel and tell him the awful news, while I got through to Will and told him I would be in his office in five minutes.

The Lady Gillian waved me through with a languid hand and kept talking on the telephone. I thought Will was going to explode when he heard the news, but he just gripped the arms of his chair and kept asking me questions I couldn't answer.

"All I can say is the client rang me just a while ago and told me to bring it forward. You should be happy; this is what you wanted."

He gave me a sharp look and asked more questions. I deflected them and emphasized I'd need some help from his ad crowd. He seemed dazed, not the calm, composed Will I'd been working with.

Finally, he got up from his desk and started pacing. I had to keep turning my head to follow his progress across the well-worn oriental rug, back and forth, back and forth. He stopped abruptly and said, "Pauline tells me you went with her to clear out Fiona's flat."

"Not to clear it out, just to help her get various insurance documents and stuff."

"I told her I would help her do that. Why did you do it?"

"Didn't she tell you? She wanted someone along who

barely knew Fiona to help her go through those things; seemed less an invasion of her privacy."

"What exactly did you find?" He turned sharply to look straight at me, eyes locking with mine.

I kept my face as impassive as possible. "She found some insurance policies and her will, I think."

"And you?"

Now I hesitated too long. He kept looking at me, making me nervous. "Nothing much."

"What is nothing much?"

"What is this, an inquisition? I checked out the bedroom and gave the stuff from her bedside table to Pauline. Ask her." That wasn't a total lie. Frankly, I was now so thoroughly ashamed of my pilfering that I wasn't about to let Will know about the draft of that letter of Fiona's and the notes about a campaign for a rival product. My first instinct that this was because of my loyalty to Sweet Whippo didn't seem honest now.

Will went back to his chair behind the desk. He leaned back, templed his fingers and just looked at me. I couldn't fathom his expression. I thought he'd be more upset about the change in plans, but instead he was grilling me about Pauline. Maybe Jane is right and he is more involved in Fiona's death than he let on. Could he have come back later that evening to see Fiona? I hadn't thought of that before.

I got up, straightened my dress carefully and headed for the door. "I'm very busy, you know, so if you don't mind, I'll get back to work."

"I do mind. Please sit down."

I paused, shrugged, and turned around. "Come on, Will, stop playing games with me. What's going on?"

Will was staring down at his fingers, his handsome face set in a frown. The silence lengthened. I watched him like a cat. Finally, he shrugged, looked up sharply at me and then waved an imperious hand. "Right, so you and Pauline did your duty by Fiona. Go back to work on your precious recipes for Sweet Whippo. I wish I had never heard of the bloody product."

"You and me, both, Will. But I am doing my level best to pull off a good campaign."

"And you and Clark have this cozy little arrangement, what?"

I decided to ignore that and made it out the door before any more words were exchanged. Yes, everybody must know about Lucille and her client.

Jane came in to my office as soon as I got there to say she had broken the news to Nigel, who had not turned a hair, but instead said he had actually in fact some recipes for us to taste and could we come to his house right now.

"Good work, Jane. I'm ready. Please see if Pauline is available. She needs to be in on this tasting." Jane reported back that Pauline had gone back to the studio but she would join us, going straight to Nigel's house. We two set off for Nigel's place. It was elegant, a Georgian townhouse on a leafy Chelsea street just off the Kings Road. He must be a very successful chef to afford this. Pauline had arrived before us and they were deep in conversation when we were shown through to the kitchen by Paul, his assistant. Nigel was elegance himself, complete with tall white toque and spotless white chef's jacket, kerchief, and traditional dark checked trousers. His shoes looked like sturdy Rockports to me, though.

We dutifully sipped sherry while Paul, not quite so flamboyant in jeans and shirt covered by a clean apron, finished the cooking. Nigel handed me a list of the five recipes he wanted to show us, each with a brief explanation of the ingredients and method of cooking. As I read, I felt a twinge of apprehension.

Rabbit Chasseur—Young rabbits, jointed, sautéed and served with prunes in cream sauce.

Squab in Ale—Young pigeons baked in ale and spices.

Mousse of Haddock and Prawns—Surrounded with curry sauce and chutney.

Soufflé of Brussels Sprouts—Garnish of chestnuts.

Rice Crème—Rice pudding with alternating layers of raspberry jam and pistachio.

"Young rabbits, jointed," was the first shock. I knew the British were fond of rabbit, but I couldn't help but picture little bunnies frolicking around. From that mental image, my mind went on to young pigeons, smaller versions of those strutting New York City birds fouling up the streets. I must have sighed or moaned because when I looked up from the list, they were all staring at me.

"Something wrong?" Nigel asked in a cold, clipped tone. "Sweet Whippo presented a challenge but I think I rose to it."

"The ideas are new to me, but nothing wrong, no."

Everyone relaxed.

Nigel signaled to Paul, who presented us with the Mousse of Haddock and Prawns, which I had to admit was good. Nigel explained how he had substituted Sweet Whippo for the double cream and garnished it with curry powder and chutney. "We cut back on fat, calories, and salt here with Whippo."

We all nodded wisely. Then we tried the Squab in Ale.

"This presented us with problems, but we managed to mix ale and Sweet Whippo together with a good chicken stock. After sautéing the squab, we covered them with julienned potato and carrots and then baked the lot," Nigel said. He was obviously pleased with his attempt.

I ate the little bird pieces, which were indeed tasty, if I could forget about the hundreds of pigeons I had seen strutting about in Trafalgar Square, being fed God knows what by tourists. Jane raved about the dish, said her mother would love it, which made Nigel and Paul beam proudly.

I braced myself for the little bunnies, but instead a soufflé was whisked out of the oven and a generous serving given to me. Now Brussels sprouts are not one of my all-time vegetable favorites, but I had to admit this soufflé was marvelous. You could hardly taste the Brussels sprouts.

I asked Nigel how the soufflés would stand up, literally, if they had to wait for any period of time at the media intro. He was ready for me.

"We considered that, but funnily enough Sweet Whippo seems to help keep the soufflé risen."

"Probably turns it to concrete later," I said.

Pauline frowned at my levity. "I think it is a very good product. So did Fiona."

We bowed our heads briefly in memory of Fiona. If the product was so good, why had Fiona been writing a plan for a rival product, according to those papers in her bedside table?

Again I braced myself for the bunnies. An old-fashioned brown pottery dish was brought forth, steam coming out.

"We could have called this dish 'Jugged Rabbit' but the guests might associate it with the classic Jugged Hare Recipe. I think 'Rabbit Chasseur' is better."

Pauline and Jane nodded. I really didn't know the difference between rabbit and hare, but I wasn't going to tell them, let alone admit I didn't really know what "Chasseur" meant either. Chase, maybe?

Paul tenderly placed a joint of the hapless animal on my plate and then spooned a red sauce over it. I waited until everyone was served and then forked in. It tasted like chicken but had a different texture. I even liked it, which made me feel guilty about the Easter Bunny.

"Sweet Whippo combines well with tomato puree," Nigel said.

He was beginning to sound like a commercial for the stuff. Chef Robert had merely said Sweet Whippo was not hard to work with. I wondered why Chef Nigel was so enthusiastic, but hoped it was sincere because it somehow seemed he was doing all this tongue-in-cheek. I felt that he didn't like the product, or me. He had this "I know something you don't know" attitude. I hoped it wasn't something bad about the product he wasn't telling me.

"I thought about Lambs' Tongues," he said to Pauline, "but decided against it." Pauline agreed with him. Lambs' Tongues I didn't want to taste.

"Now for the pudding," he announced.

Pauline and Jane sat up straight in their chairs, for all the world like schoolchildren, as Paul put down a molded mound of what looked like rice pudding to me. Diner food, yet.

"Sweet Whippo combined well with jelly—gelatin to you—" he said with a nod toward me, "and with jam. I call this 'Rice Crème.' " When Paul cut a slice from the mold, I could see it had one layer of red Jell-O–looking stuff and one of pistachios. Very colorful.

Again we ate. Jane said she thought it would be a simple and easy idea for the British housewife to do. She and Pauline both took an extra slice. The British do have that sweet tooth, I thought, when I looked at all the jams and jellies on the shelves.

When we looked at the recipes, I suddenly realized that Nigel was working in metric and Robert in U.S. measurements.

"Will Robert have to translate his U.S. measurements into metric?" I asked. "He can, of course."

There was a silence and then Pauline spoke. "Since this is a contest between an American chef and his British counterpart, I think we should show both styles. There are still people in Britain who don't like metric measure, mainly older people, of course. Many recipes are still given in both measurements."

"Okay, Pauline, I'll check with Robert. I know he was trained in both methods so there should be no problem."

"I'll get on with recipe development," Nigel said. "There's still time. You realize, of course, that I've kept the recipes simple, easy for the British housewife. I'm much more used to more elaborate recipe development. I hope people understand."

He obviously felt he was compromising his reputation as a great chef, trained in Paris, to stoop to Sweet Whippo. But he was doing it.

Pauline nodded and murmured that of course people in the food world would understand.

"I'll see that you get another case of Sweet Whippo," Pauline added.

All this cooperation from Pauline intrigued me. After a cup of tea to clear our palates, we got ready to leave, but Nigel asked me to join him for a private chat. I left Jane and Pauline talking to each other as Paul loaded the dishwasher. Nigel and I walked into the sitting room.

"Will Hammersmith rang me yesterday to see how I was progressing. He told me to take my time creating these recipes as he wanted to be sure they would be good. I must say

117

I was put off a bit, as I didn't feel my ability should be questioned."

"It isn't, and now you know that we must all work even faster," I said.

"I just thought I'd let you know that Hammersmith is taking a very personal interest in my work. Do you know why?"

Why was he telling me this?

"No, but I'll talk to Will," I said.

He nodded, turned to lead the way back into the kitchen and said, "Great pity about Fiona Gordon. So talented."

"You knew her, of course."

"Oh yes, indeed. Quite well, actually. You know how it is in this field. Everyone knows everyone. Braxton Clark used to bring her round to some of my little do's and then of course Fiona and I have done work together on the road." He smiled smugly.

I didn't like that smile. Was that a dig about Braxton Clark? I shrugged, collected Jane and Pauline and we taxied back to the office. I don't think either of them noticed my silence. Nigel and Fiona? Did Nigel drive a Jaguar?

I walked into my office and there it was again. The little buff-colored envelope. This time the note said, "You have only a few days left before something really nasty happens to you. Bugger off now!"

Chapter 14

To tell you the truth, I was so tired and so full of Sweet Whippo'd food that I crumpled up the envelope and said aloud, "You win, whoever you are. I will bugger off. Just give me a few days more!"

But I changed my mind when the telephone rang just then and it was Brack. I calmed down as I told him the day's events. I didn't tell him about the note, but I did tell him the good news about the chefs. We talked; he convinced me he was still interested in me personally. No, I would not bugger off even if I couldn't see Brack for too long a time. I put that crumpled note in my bag to take home.

The next two weeks were nonstop hell. I worked until nine every night. On the nights when Jane wasn't working with me—a comforting presence next door—I kept my office door locked. I told myself it was silly, but I took no chances. Suppose that note writer was also a stalker? He—or she—could also be a poisoner of chocolates. Yes, those truffles were still in my freezer. I was hesitant to find out where to send them for a lab test for fear someone at the office would hear about it. That someone could be the poisoner—or I could just be making all this up and the chocolates were delivered to me by mistake. I began thinking I was making it all up.

At this time of year the evenings were light until almost ten o'clock so I still strolled back to the flat after work, looking behind me often. It broke my heart to see the glorious London twilights, the fading sunlight golden on the old houses, all the trees in leaf, the roses in bloom, and there I was stuck with all that damn work. I did take one weekend off and indulged myself in the theater, a concert and just watching the London world go by, sitting on a bench in Hyde Park. Jane and her boyfriend asked me to join them in hill walking, but that somehow didn't appeal to me. I missed Brack, but did he miss me?

London Office, to its credit, rallied round and the chosen press and media got invited, food photographs got taken and media kits printed and the problems of serving and heating the food dealt with. The overtime put in by London staff played havoc with my budget, so I went straight to John Bowen, head of the office and told him the story. He assured me he would get the extra money from the client. That helped me when Will started carping about costs by impersonal memos. Otherwise he ignored me.

Every day I braced myself to find another nasty note, but curiously, in spite of that threat of something bad happening to me in the next few days, nothing did. That is, if you discount trouble with photographs, trouble with copywriters, trouble with printers and long, involved, troubled conversations with my two chefs, who kept changing the recipes.

Finally, the big day was upon us.

The Argyle Club, an exclusive men's club in London, was chosen for the media introduction luncheon because of the snob appeal and because it had a great kitchen. John Bowen was on its board of directors and since he knew that the club always needed money, he convinced it to let the great unwashed in, at least into one foyer, dining room, kitchen and bathrooms.

Jane and Pauline and I did the final taste testings, and to our great relief, both chefs had come up with some real winners. Sweet Whippo might well turn out to be the savior of the contemporary stomach.

Pauline had remained strangely silent about her crusade to prove that Fiona had been done in. I brought it up a couple of times, but she told me that she really didn't need my help anymore as she had worked out her own plan. No matter how I quizzed her about this—trying not to show my real curiosity—she remained close-mouthed. I just hoped her own plan was not something weird, as she was so mysterious about it. Obviously, I had been dropped from her master plan.

What was Brack doing all this time? He was on the phone to me every night and since he sounded as interested in me as in the media introduction, it gave me hope. With the direct dialing system I could never figure out where he was calling from and he had vague answers to my questions about his whereabouts.

"Not to worry, Lulu, I'll be at your big luncheon."

"Are you coming in the night before?" I asked. "If so, will I see you? I need desperately to show you the setup. We could go over everything the night before."

What I meant was I needed desperately to have him in my bed. I was feeling all alone in a foreign country. Danny must have sensed something was going on between me and someone here because his calls were more frequent and lasted longer. He even mentioned something about flying over for a long weekend. I discouraged him, telling him I was too busy with this launch for any social life. Also, I wouldn't know how I really felt about Brack until this launch was over and we could be together again.

"I have the utmost confidence in your work, so that won't really be necessary," Brack countered, when I urged him to get back earlier. "But reserve the night of the big occasion for me, will you, and the weekend?"

All was not lost.

I didn't sleep very well the night before the introduction, and I had disturbing dreams about things going wrong at the luncheon. I'd never yet had a media introduction where something *didn't* get fouled up, so I wanted to be ready.

Jane, Pauline and I, loaded with press materials, made our way into the club very early in the morning of the big day to make absolutely sure of absolutely everything. When the chefs arrived, they were directed to separate ends of the big kitchen. Pauline was assigned to keep them apart and to make sure they had everything they needed in food and equipment. Things got a bit sticky when Justin, the executive chef of the Argyle club, sauntered in, greeted Nigel cordially and chatted him up. Robert scowled at this favoritism, but Pauline assured him that the two British chefs had known each other for years. She dragged Chef Justin over and made him talk to Robert, too. Pauline was turning out to be our guardian angel with chefs, even though she was so nervous that I figured she was one step ahead of a running fit. I was even relieved when she smiled sheepishly when I saw her popping something in her mouth and told me she thought she'd take a pill or two to calm her nerves. I almost asked her for one for *my* nerves.

Justin had assigned two each of his own sous chefs to Nigel and Robert, but he kept his beady eye on them, standing there majestically in his starched white toque, spotless white jacket and the traditional checked trousers.

Our chefs were in uniform, too, but their jackets were fast getting spattered with food of all colors.

Will walked into the kitchen just as everyone was getting frantic, and he took it upon himself to do his "coach talking to the lads before the game" routine. He kept getting in the chefs' way until Robert managed to drop some hot gravy on Will's handmade polished shoes and he decided to move back out of the line of fire.

"Everything on a fine yarn, is it, Lucille?" Will asked, as he wiped off his shoes with a clean kitchen towel. "That's an expression we use in our Navy."

"Everything's coming together just peachy keen," I answered. "That's an expression we use in New York."

Will raised his eyebrows, gave me a disdainful look but I couldn't get rid of him. He stayed right by my side.

The wait staff arrived and stood at attention while Jane and I gave them orders. We had actually run through this routine with them a few days ago, but it never hurts to polish. Will watched this with interest, nodding wisely at times, just as if he knew what was going on. I barely restrained myself from picking up one of the big copper pots and braining him, and my displeasure must have been apparent, because when I looked around a little later, he had attached himself to Pauline, at the far end of the kitchen, who was listening to him, head cocked to one side. When he saw me looking at them, he smiled, waved, gave a thumbs-up signal and departed through the door to the dining room, nearly colliding with Brack on his way into the kitchen. Will put his hand on Brack's arm and tried to stop him, but he frowned, shook Will's arm off and continued toward me.

We were very businesslike as we shook hands, but we couldn't stop grinning at each other. He talked to Nigel and

Robert, separately, then the maitre d' and Justin, while I stood by.

"Everything seems very much under control," he said. "I'm looking forward to this."

"I'm not," I said, groaning. "But I know, I know, stiff upper lip and all that British jazz."

Brack smiled at me and actually put his arm around me, squeezing me. In public! It was brief, but I took enormous strength from that, enough strength to face the next two hours.

This luncheon was not a huge one, on the advice of those in charge of invitations. "We'll start with the very top food people from newspapers, magazines, radio and television here in London, along with a handful of celebrity chefs," the media expert had said. "They'll tell you exactly what they think, no holds barred, and we can carry on from there. I'm told they rather liked the idea of an American chef and a British chef competing in a friendly way with this new product."

Our setup was that each chef would prepare an appetizer, a fish course, a meat or poultry dish plus one vegetable, all to be served to the food experts in small portions. Each guest had a menu which gave the name of each recipe, the nutritional analysis, and how Sweet Whippo had been used to cut down on the fat, sugar, salt and calories. No genetic modification. Never. And it was emphasized that this was not a diet pill or a formula for use by the seriously obese. Just a new product for the housewife to use to feed her family the best way. Each diner also had a scorecard to use to rate the dishes. Then the guests would get up (if they could still walk) and go to two buffet tables loaded with desserts, three each from both chefs for them to sample. Appropriate wines went with each course. Talk about a feeding frenzy!

Jane and I took one last look around the kitchen before we went into the dining room. The chefs were busy slinging pots and pans around, Pauline was running back and forth between them and the waiters were organizing trays and plates.

"If this meal doesn't kill off these experts, we'll be lucky," I said to Jane. "Look at all that food, all made with our glop. I can't believe they won't take one taste and run for the loo."

"You're sweating, Lucille," she said quietly. "Your face is all shiny."

"I might have to run for the loo, myself, and soon," I said, wiping my face hastily as we went to view the elegant room, with its starched white tablecloths, centerpieces of freesias and anemones, place settings of silver and sparkling glasses. We checked the place cards carefully. So far everything was as planned.

Jane and I pasted smiles on our faces and hurried into the dark paneled foyer to greet the guests, who were to be softened up with plenty of champagne, wine and spirits before their ordeal. Brack and Will had already stationed themselves there, along with John Bowen. Brack was looking over his notes for his brief speech about Sweet Whippo just before the desserts were rolled out. Pauline had insisted upon staying in the kitchen to help the chefs, but I had assured her that Brack would certainly put something in his remarks about Fiona and her great and now much-missed contribution to the food world and her unfortunate accidental death. Jane was good about introducing me to the powerful British food types, who seemed harmless enough at this point. But wait until they got hold of Robert's barbecued ribs or Nigel's bunnies.

"Your face is perspiring again," Jane warned me.

125

"Powder would help."

On the way back from the ladies' room, I glanced at my watch to discover it was already ten minutes past the designated time to seat the guests. I headed for the kitchen to check the delay and there I found Pauline sitting on the floor, legs straight out, her face pale, her hands shaking. The chefs and wait staff were standing over her, and Robert had a hand on her shoulder.

"Oh God, what's wrong with her?"

"She ate one of the desserts," Robert said.

I kept myself from collapsing by hanging on to one of the steel tables until I had enough strength to lean over her.

"Pauline, what's wrong? What happened?"

She looked up at me with a pathetic face. "I just thought I'd try a rice crème, you know, the ones Nigel made, for a final tasting before they took them into the dining room, and right away I came all over funny."

Nigel's face was stony. He had a big knife in his hand and I hoped he would not lose his temper at this insult.

"Did anyone else try one?" I asked.

"Are you bonkers?" one of the sous chefs muttered. "Look at her."

Bonkers or not, I had to find out for myself if anything was wrong before those foodies in the dining room put those rice creams into their stomachs, so I walked over to the table where the desserts were, found a tray of the culprits, took a spoon, scooped up a goodly amount of one and ate it. The kitchen was deadly silent as they all watched me. I swallowed, swallowed again and looked around. The faces were all turned to me, all waiting to see me collapse. A long, long minute went by. I could taste sweetness in my mouth, but that's all. I shrugged. The faces relaxed.

"Nothing wrong with that rice crème," I said. "You

must have been too nervous, Pauline, and your stomach
was upset. Go sit down somewhere and take another one of
your pills. As for the rest of you, please, please, get this
show on the road or I will take one of these knives and personally cut somebody's throat right now." I tried to smile to
soften the words.

Pauline gave me a weak smile, let Robert help her up
and wobbled down to the far end of the kitchen to sit
bravely on a chair, head hanging down, hands neatly folded
in her lap.

Nigel looked over at me, rolled his eyes and shook his
head.

"One down, and lots more to go," I distinctly heard
someone remark as I walked through the kitchen door.

Back in the foyer, I put on my public relations face and
signaled to Jane to get the guests into the dining room. Before I could join them, a television team showed up unex-
pectedly and asked to go into the kitchen and film the chefs
at work. I was livid because they hadn't let us know their
plans. Then I had the awful thought that they might have
heard that there was a chance of death or deathly illness
showing up at this party. I was barely able to speak coher-
ently as I led them there, introduced them to Robert and
Nigel, went back into the dining room, sent Jane into the
kitchen to handle the TV team (murmuring that Pauline
wasn't feeling well) and found my table. My legs, out of
sight under the white linen draped tablecloths, would not
stop shaking. My fertile imagination started working. Suppose Sweet Whippo turned out to be lethal to extra-sensitive
stomachs? Would any of these guests follow Pauline's ex-
ample? Suppose there really *was* something wrong with
Nigel's rice crèmes? My own stomach began feeling queasy.
Should I cut and run right now before the whole debacle

started? I half rose from my chair, but then sank back down. No, not in front of Brack.

My hands under the tablecloth were gripped together as I smiled brilliantly around my table as the waiters starting serving the appetizers. With a shaking hand, I fed myself a bit of Robert's Cheese Puff in Balsamic Dill Sauce and choked it down. I still wasn't convinced that there wasn't something in Sweet Whippo which could turn these recipes into food from hell. Nigel's Curried Leek Soup which followed went down more smoothly. I watched intently as the people at my table ate their appetizers, consulted their menus and made little marks on their scorecards.

"Dear lady, don't be so apprehensive," the man on my right said to me. "We aren't eating poison." He smiled round the table and the others smiled back.

A lot he knew.

"Dear lady," he went on, looking and sounding more and more like John Gielgud, "I've been to many, many of these press do's and so far, no one I know has died."

"This can be a first," I said. Polite titters around the table.

As the fish course was served, there were appreciative murmurs about Robert's Maryland Crab Cakes—they had been Sweet Whippo'd into light fluffy cakes. Pencils busily scratched away. Nigel's Salmon Terrine was good but not spectacularly so, I heard one woman confide to her neighbor.

I washed everything down with wine, so much wine that the waiter filling my glass looked sharply at me. At least my legs had stopped shaking, but any more wine and they might not support me. I gulped down some water.

Nigel's Rabbit Chasseur was a hit, I could tell, as people fearlessly forked into those helpless little legs and bodies.

The Texas Barbecued Ribs recipe was made with small neat ribs, but the food experts of Great Britain obviously didn't like picking up drippy pieces of meat with their bare hands, and most attacked them with knife and fork, ruining the whole informal food idea. Jane's idea of waiters handing out hot, moistened towels after the course was a lifesaver. Jane herself had returned to the dining room and gave me a big smile and nod, so I assumed that the TV shoot had gone well.

The vegetables accompanying these main courses were just okay to my taste. I mean, who can really be thrilled with a Puree of Brussels Sprouts and Potatoes (Nigel's new idea) or Corn Fritters (Robert's specialty)? But they were dutifully eaten and judged.

Champagne was brought out and handed round, and Brack got up and made a mercifully short and amusing speech about the new product. He gave Fiona Gordon a lot of credit for her work with Sweet Whippo and that brought approving murmurs from the guests. As the dessert buffet tables were being rolled in, I decided to go and alert the chefs to get ready for their personal appearances. I staggered slightly as I got up from the table and Brack was immediately at my side, holding my arm. Firmly.

"I must go get the chefs."

"I'll go with you."

The kitchen looked like a bomb had dropped, with dirty pots and pans and food scattered all around. The TV crew had gone and Nigel and Robert and Chef Justin and all the sous chefs were sitting at a table, open bottles of wine and champagne in front of them. Robert's white jacket was splattered with barbecue sauce, something green, a few shreds of what I hoped was crab and Nigel seemed to have a river of different colored food running down his front. The sous chefs' jackets looked like they had fallen head first into a vat of Sweet Whippo. Chef Justin's white front was still white, but then he hadn't had to do any cooking. The toques lay on the table, crushed. Pauline was not to be seen and when I asked about her they said she'd gone off to lie down.

"Good show, men," Braxton said, and the chefs held their glasses up in reply. I swear they were all drunk. I envied them.

"Nigel and Robert, and all you chefs, you did a wonderful job," I said. "Wonderful. Now, I think perhaps my star chefs should put on some clean jackets and toques and get ready for your appearance in the dining room soon to hear the results of the judging. I wish you both could win."

Neither Robert nor Nigel seemed at all anxious about the results. Now I knew they were drunk. Brack gently took my arm and we walked toward the dining room. At the door, he pulled me aside and kissed me, hard.

"That's for doing such a bang-up job. There'll be more tonight," he said, smiling at me. I heard someone in the kitchen give a polite snort, but I didn't care.

From the looks of the guests back in the dining room, the desserts had been the biggest hit. The plates of goodies which had been so carefully decorated were practically empty. Sweet Whippo had come into its own. Two of the celebrated food experts were reading off the scorecards to Jane, who was smiling and nodding and writing down the results. Brack was helping her as coffee and brandy was being handed round to the guests.

When they finished, Jane came over to me and whispered, "We did it, Lucille, we actually did it! They loved the stuff."

"Nobody's died yet?" I asked.

"Nobody's even turned green," she assured me.

"Which chef won?" I asked.

"It was a tie!"

"Oh, come on, Jane, don't be stupid. It can't be a tie."

"Believe it or not, it was so close that Braxton Clark said he was going to call it a tie."

"That eliminates mayhem, anyhow, but do you think the press will accept that?"

"Give them more brandy and they'll accept anything," Jane said, happily.

When the chefs were brought in and the results announced, there were good-natured boos, laughs and applause.

Nigel stepped forward and said, "I just thought you lot would like to know that Chef Robert and I have had a little talk in that kitchen, and we have decided we would like to open a restaurant together, here in London. We will feature both British and American specialties, of course."

They had to be drunk.

"But we won't call it Sweet Whippo," Robert stepped forward and said. "I promise."

The laughter broke up the party and the guests started slowly filing out, picking up the media kits from the table in the foyer.

I looked around for Will so I could gloat, but before I could spot him I saw Pauline coming from the kitchen door, stumbling and sobbing, heading right for me. I went forward and grabbed her, trying to hold her up, but she was too heavy, her legs buckling under her

"Lucille, Lucille, I'm so sick. I know it's poison, I just know it." She sagged even lower and I could barely hold her. She was sobbing and muttering something I couldn't quite hear.

Will appeared at my side and helped me pull her to her feet. When she turned and saw him, she cried out, "What have you done to me?"

"Pauline, Pauline, please. Tell us what happened, what's wrong," I begged.

But she sank down to the floor again, head bowed, sobbing away. Then she moaned and fell to one side, where she lay, not moving.

Chapter 15

Brack appeared suddenly and took over the situation. Aside from leaning over Pauline and putting a tentative hand on her shoulder, I couldn't seem to function. But then she moved and struggled to sit up. I was weak with relief.

"Pauline, Pauline, are you all right?" I asked as she grabbed my hand.

"Help me up," she ordered. She took a deep shuddering breath and stopped weeping. Brack and Will helped to drag her to her feet. Brack was murmuring encouragement, but Will was totally silent, holding on to her shoulder, staring at her. I had my arms around her, trying to keep her upright.

"Let's get her to hospital," Brack said. "My car is in the drive and the hospital is just around the corner. I think that's the best thing." He gave me a look that said, "Right Away!"

Pauline twisted in my arms, looked up at him and said, her voice quavering, "Was it you? Did you try to shut me up?" Then she started whimpering and muttering. I figured she had finally flipped.

Brack ignored her question, taking her arms in a strong grip, nodding to me to let go, and telling Will to hold on tightly. Together, they walked her back into the kitchen, out its back door, all of them staggering as they maneuvered the steps and finally to Brack's big car. I followed as closely as I could, trying to hear what she was saying under her breath, but I couldn't make much sense of it. We manhandled her into the backseat and I got in beside her. She sat upright, then, turning to look at me, a look I couldn't fathom, but I was only thankful that at least she had stopped that weeping and muttering. Brack closed the door and told Will to follow us in his own car. Will simply nodded. He still looked stunned.

The drive to the hospital and into the area by the Emergency Room entrance was mercifully short. Miraculously, the Emergency Room had only a scattering of people in it. A nurse and an orderly relieved us of Pauline, who stumbled with them into an adjoining room. Brack and I stayed behind while I explained to the reception clerk what had happened. She kept nodding, speaking in low, calm tones, writing away, then asking us to wait, please.

Will burst into the room and demanded to know what was wrong with Pauline. "Was it poison?" he asked in a too-loud voice. He had obviously come out of his shock. The people sitting around looked up with undisguised interest at his question.

"We don't know yet, Will," Brack said quietly. "She cried out about poison, but we'll know more later. Sit down here." We all three found seats and joined the waiting people. Brack stared straight ahead, but Will shifted around in his seat so he could look at me. He had a stubborn, almost gloating look on his face.

"She's gone round the twist, you know. Totally unstable woman."

"You're all heart, Will," I said. I had a hangover from all that wine, I was bone tired and I didn't want to listen to him running poor Pauline down. In the brief silence that followed, I was turning over and over in my mind Pauline's words to Brack. She had said, "Was it you? Did you try to shut me up?" What could she mean by that? But she had also said to Will, "What have you done to me?" That was after she had said, "Lucille, Lucille, I'm so sick, I know it's poison." Where had she got hold of poison? I remembered that the chefs had told me that Pauline had gone to lie down. Had the poor woman taken some poison? Why? Please, God, don't let it be Sweet Whippo.

Will shifted restlessly in his chair and spoke again. "She's bonkers, that's all," he insisted. "Nobody poisoned her."

"We'll soon know," Brack said. He didn't look at me, didn't say anything, just sat there, face grim, staring straight ahead. We must have been a good sideshow for the other waiting people. I didn't have the nerve to tell them about Pauline's first stomach upset.

There was more silence, each of us obviously lost in thought, until I spoke my thoughts. "It can't be Sweet Whippo; nobody else got sick."

"Yet," muttered Will.

"Nonsense," said Brack firmly. "That won't wash, Will. We've tested and tested for months. I figure Pauline took something herself, probably tranquilizers for her nerves, and then added booze."

Will shook his head. "She had a chemical reaction to something in that product."

"Shut up, Will," Brack said, his voice rising. Others in the room looked up at us curiously. His face was flushed and I thought there might possibly be a fight. In fact, I rather hoped so. I'd have liked to see Will pushed around by Brack.

Before that could happen, a young man dressed in hospital garb came out of the room that Pauline had disappeared in and said something to the reception clerk. Then he disappeared down a hall. I jumped up, went over to the reception clerk and asked her what was going on with Pauline now, and after a hard stare at me, she took me over to another desk where yet another nurse was sitting, handed her a clipboard and left me there.

In those quiet tones the British use to tell you about disasters and death, that nurse told me that the patient was getting a stomach lavage and would then be held overnight for observation. Stomach lavage—a fancy word for getting all that great food and champagne in her stomach pumped out.

"Can I see her any time soon? She doesn't have any family here in London and she lives alone," I said. I really didn't know if that was the complete truth, but I had to find out what was wrong with her.

"Come back in two hours and notify her GP in the meantime," was the crisp retort. I nodded, even though I had no idea who Pauline's doctor was, and told her I would be back and then rejoined the two men to repeat that information.

"Brack, there's no point in all of us trailing back here. Why don't you and Will go on to your offices and I'll go back to the club and finish up odds and ends with Jane. I'll come back in a couple of hours and see how Pauline is." I didn't want them around until I had a chance to talk to Pauline.

"I'll be back, too," Will announced.

Not if I could help it.

Brack pulled me aside and said, "I don't think I'll be back as I have a job to do which will take some time. But I'll be by your flat about seven. It was a great party and you did a bang-up job. See you at seven, I promise."

Then he turned to Will and said, "Come with me, Will. You and I are going to have a long, long talk."

Will shook his head and turned to walk away, but Brack grabbed his arm. "I said, come with me." Will shrugged and went with him. I watched them disappear. They seemed to have forgotten I was even there.

Back at the Argyle Club, the kitchen staff was still cleaning up, while our chefs and Jane were sitting at a stainless steel table, polishing off the champagne, the extra press materials stacked precariously on one end of the table. I practically fell into a chair, took the glass of champagne Robert handed me and started answering their questions about Pauline. I merely said Pauline got very sick very quickly and we decided to take her straight to the hospital.

Robert wanted to dash to the hospital right away and told me he was upset that we hadn't told him what was happening as he would have gone to the hospital with us. Nigel nodded in agreement.

"We saw all that commotion, but we were saying goodbye to some people and by the time we got there to see what was wrong, you were walking Pauline out the door. Will wouldn't tell us what was going on. We didn't know you had taken her to the hospital," Robert complained.

It's true I had completely forgotten about the chefs and Jane in all the confusion. I told him to sit tight and he could go back with me in a couple of hours. He subsided gloomily. I hadn't realized he and Pauline were such friends. Had I missed something somewhere?

Nigel kept quizzing me. He wanted to know why the hospital was pumping her stomach out, what had she eaten at the party, what had she said to us on the way to the hospital.

"I heard *she* said she had been poisoned, and I sincerely hope she didn't accuse *me* of doing that," Nigel said. "I don't remember what the poor woman was eating here in the kitchen while we were so busy, and I know she thought that rice crème was off, but that doesn't make sense. No one else complained or suffered any ill effects from my cooking." He was obviously on the defensive. Somebody must have heard what Pauline had cried out and was spreading it around.

"Why should she accuse *you*?" Robert asked.

Nigel looked hard at Robert, but answered flippantly, "The dear girl was always a bit crackers, you know, probably thought I was feeding arsenic to her."

"What do you mean, 'crackers'?" Robert demanded.

"I mean, she was obsessed with Fiona's death, old man, and kept after me to do things the way Fiona would have done them." He turned and looked at me, one eyebrow raised. "Perhaps you didn't know this, Lucille, but she also kept after me to help her find Fiona's killer. Killer, indeed, the poor woman just lost her balance and fell, of course."

I turned to Robert. "Did she talk to you, too, about Fiona's death and if so, why wasn't I told?"

Robert looked shamefaced. "You had enough on your mind, Lucille. I just listened to her and then went on about my business. I know she was terribly upset about this woman's death, but I wasn't even over here when that happened."

You're only over here because it happened, I wanted to say to him, but kept my mouth shut. So this was what Pauline had meant about her own plans. Getting my chefs involved.

Nigel asked, "What hospital is she in? I will just nip by on my way home and see her. I want her to know I did not poison her. Lucille, I did notice that she was popping pills, one after the other. What was she taking?"

"Something for her nerves, I guess. But she doesn't need any company for a while, so postpone your visit, Nigel." I gave a big sigh, put aside the champagne glass and said, "Come on, Jane, let's get our stuff back to the office. I'll go to the hospital from there."

Nigel shrugged and said, "Just a thought. I'll ring her tomorrow." He started taking off his chef's jacket, which still had stains down the front, and picking up some of his equipment.

Robert followed suit, shaking out his jacket and folding it. I turned and thanked all the staff again while Robert then helped us gather up the leftover media folders, saying he would join us later. Back at the office, we had to spend the next hour telling various members of the staff about the luncheon, its success, and fending off questions about Pauline's illness. Jane and I had agreed on the way back just to say that Pauline knew she was getting sick but that she had gallantly stayed through the luncheon. No mention of poison.

Robert strolled in then, accepted the congratulations of the assembled staff, one by one, and then announced to me that he could not go home until he had gone with me to the hospital to see Pauline. I gave up, agreed, but sent him down to the kitchens to do some work while we waited another hour or so. I was too tired to do anything but sit at my desk, head in my hands, trying not to think. Finally we left for the hospital, where the receptionist remembered me and even seemed pleased to see me.

"Miss Greene has been asking for you, repeatedly," she announced.

"For me?"

She talked to someone on an intercom and a nurse appeared.

"Follow me," she ordered. "Just you. You stay here," she told Robert firmly, and stepped off quickly down a corridor. I looked at Robert's disappointed face, shrugged, patted him on the arm and said I'd be only a minute, then I followed her at a fast clip.

The nurse led me into a large room. There were three beds with women patients tucked up in them, whose eyes followed our progress to a curtained-off cubicle in a corner. The nurse pulled the curtains back, motioned me to a wooden chair next to the bed, saying, "Please don't tire the patient. She's already had one visitor that I had to chase out!"

"Who?" I asked her, but she ignored me, whipped the curtains back around with a practiced hand, and departed.

Pauline looked ghastly, face so pale her freckles stood out, blue eyes sunk back in her head, straw-colored hair straggling over one cheek. She stared at me, mouth opening and closing silently.

"Who was just here, Pauline?"

She didn't answer, just stared at me, eyes awash in tears, face twisted in pain.

"Never mind, Pauline," I said. "You'll soon be all right, I'm sure." I leaned forward to pat her shoulder and smile a confident smile.

She shook her head then and tried to sit up. In low, sad tones, she said, "I have to get this off my chest while I still have time." She struggled to a half sitting position. I tried to help her but she shrugged me away. What did she mean "while she still had time?"

She took a deep breath and said, "Those notes you got. *I* sent them. I mean, Fiona and I sent the first one, just as a joke, you know. We laughed about it. She loved practical jokes."

I stared at her.

"Then, after Fiona died, I decided to keep on sending them. In her memory, you understand. Now I'm sorry. I shouldn't have done it. It was silly."

"It was cruel," I said.

She nodded her head, giving me such a sad and pitiful look that I even felt a little guilty, saying this to a sick woman.

"How about the chocolates?" I couldn't resist asking, no matter how sick she was. "Was that Fiona's idea, too?"

"Chocolates?" Pauline looked puzzled. "What chocolates?"

She gave an enormous sigh, then fell back again on the pillow. "It was wrong, terribly wrong to tease you that way. Can you forgive me? I must be forgiven or I won't sleep. They want me to stay overnight because I live alone and there's no one there to look after me. Fiona would have looked after me." She started weeping silently.

I sat motionless for a moment. Then I tried again. "Of course I forgive you. It doesn't matter now, Pauline. Nobody knows about those notes because I didn't tell anyone. Just try to get well." I tried a forgiving smile on her, hoping to salve that conscience of hers, but she didn't respond. Then I wished I had had a tape recorder hidden on me. This was too good a story line for a mystery, but nobody would believe me that dear Fiona and good old Pauline had pulled this trick. What kind of detective was I if I didn't think about these things? Or was I callous?

"That's not all," she said.

I felt a chill, a definite chill.

"It's Will Hammersmith. Fiona told him about the first

note and he guessed I sent the others, and he told me he would tell you—and John Bowen—if I didn't do what he wanted me to."

"And what was that?"

"You won't believe this. He wanted me to find out if there was some sort of product that could be added to one of the dishes at the party which would make people just slightly sick. He said it would serve you right for pretending that the chef's cook-off was to honor Fiona. Of course I refused, but now I think *he* did find out about some product and put it on that one rice crème I ate. He was hanging around that table where they were. He could have done it. That's why I got sick."

I simply didn't know what to believe. Would Will actually do something like that? And other people had eaten those crèmes and had not gotten sick. No, I wouldn't accept that. I was beginning to believe that she was getting more and more weird.

"Pauline, are you telling me the truth? Did Will really ask you to put something into the desserts, uh sweets, uh puddings, whatever?" I was beginning to sound slightly off my head myself. "Are you absolutely sure? This is quite an accusation."

My voice had risen and sounded loud, even to me. The curtains were pulled back quickly and the nurse stood there, glaring at me, shaking her head in disapproval.

"You must go," she ordered.

"No, no, please, please," Pauline cried weakly.

"Lower your voice," the nurse said to me. We stared at each other. She was dressed in this dark blue dress with a tight black belt and black stockings topped by a mass of red hair. She was considerably shorter than I was and much younger, but she made it plain she was in charge.

"I'm sorry," I said. After another reproving shake of the head, she departed, closing the curtains behind her. I thought about what Pauline had just said. No wonder she accused Will of poisoning her. But why would she ask Brack if he had tried to shut her up? What was his part in this? She had accused him of killing Fiona and now she was accusing him of coming after her.

"No, I must tell you, I must tell you . . ." Her voice trailed off and she closed her eyes. Then she opened them, stared at me and reached out and grabbed my arm with a shaky hand. "Please, listen to me. There's more." She stared at me so intently that I actually felt goose pimples start up on both my arms. There was this uneasy silence for too long a time.

When she didn't say anything, I prompted her. "Why did Will want to sabotage the press launch, Pauline? I mean, he's involved in this campaign, too. You're sure it was just to get back at me?"

Pauline leaned forward, her face a few inches from mine, breathing jerkily. I got worried, really worried, about her. Then I heard someone moving about outside the curtain and I hoped it was the dragon nurse, waiting to pounce. I needed some help here. But the curtains hung motionless.

Pauline leaned back a little and said, "Will Hammersmith loved Fiona, you know, would do anything for her. But I couldn't do anything like that. I think he was very angry with me when I refused, but I was even angrier because he wouldn't help me find Fiona's killer. He laughed at me and said there was no killer, that she had just tripped and fallen. So I decided to do something more on my own. Yesterday I sent a letter to him, and I sent the same letter to Mr. Clark and to two other men that had been Fiona's lovers. In fact," and here that determined look came back to her mouth, "I also sent a copy of the letter to that policeman—Reid—in charge of the case. I wanted them all to know that I was not giving up, I was not accepting that stupid theory that Fiona accidentally fell. I was quite firm in those letters. I told them that each one of them was under suspicion and must prove to the police that he had a good alibi or be accused of murder."

I was stunned into silence. Pauline and I stared at each other and then she smiled this smug smile. I swear I could hear someone breathing, someone standing right outside that curtain. Now I was getting paranoid.

Finally I found my voice. "You sent letters to these men—to Will and to Braxton Clark—and said they were under suspicion. Who were the other two men?"

Just then the curtain was pulled back again and a man appeared, dressed in a white coat, the white contrasting with his dark skin. The nurse stood next to him now, and by her deferential attitude, I figured out this was Pauline's doctor. He gave me a sharp look, then leaned over to look at her.

"Ah, we are coming along nicely," he said.

Pauline just groaned and closed her eyes, her hand on my arm.

"Perhaps I should leave," I suggested and tried to gently dislodge Pauline's hand. She wouldn't let go.

He nodded.

"Uh, Pauline, we'll talk another time, when you are well."

She cried out something and grabbed my arm. I stood there, not knowing what I should do.

"Please wait in the hall," the doctor said and I obeyed, gently dislodging Pauline's clammy hand from my arm. I was eager to fight my way out of those clinging, dingy white curtains. I walked quickly to the door and opened it, without looking back at the curtained bed. I sat down on a bench just outside the door, my brain trying to take all this in. What kind of hornet's nest had Pauline stirred up with those accusing letters? She'd sent them yesterday.

The doctor appeared shortly after and sat down beside me. He looked at me gravely over his wire-rimmed spectacles.

"Is she seriously ill?" I asked. "She's not making much sense."

"Oh my, no," he said with a little smile. "She will recover and soon."

"But I thought . . ."

"In her stomach she had too many Valiums, too much champagne, too much rich food eaten too quickly."

He smiled at me, apparently amused at my puzzled stare.

"She said she was poisoned," I offered.

"No poison. Why did she think poison?"

"I think she was confused. You say it was just Valium and champagne."

"Very confused, but that is not unusual," the doctor admitted. "She can go home tomorrow. You are a relative? You will collect her?"

"No, just a colleague. We work together."

He seemed surprised at my remark, and I realized that the nosy nurse had probably told him that Pauline had asked specifically for me. But I would indeed collect Pauline from the hospital tomorrow, take her home and find out more about these letters and if Will Hammersmith had indeed tried to sabotage my luncheon. I assured the doctor that I would ring tomorrow morning and make the arrangements. The nurse conveniently appeared and I asked her to tell Pauline that I would be there to take her home tomorrow. She actually smiled at me and walked with me back to reception.

Robert was waiting anxiously in reception, but the nurse would not let him go to Pauline and was so adamant about it that he finally gave up and we went back to the office. Everybody had gone home and only faithful Jane was there, so I told her what the doctor had said about too many Valiums, too much champagne. Jane shook her head.

"She came damn near ruining our party. Thank God she waited until the very end to get sick. Think of what could have happened, what a field day for the press and telly." She patted her stomach and said, "If I don't get home soon, I may join her in that hospital. It's been one hell of a day."

I nodded wearily, urged Robert to give up and go home, that he could see Pauline tomorrow, and sat at my desk. I rang Will's office, but no one answered. I was so tired that I couldn't think straight, but my brain wouldn't let go. Will must have enjoyed thinking about me getting those nasty notes, but what about Pauline's accusing letter to him? And for that matter, what about that same letter to Brack? Had he gotten it yet and if he had, how could I find out what was in it? And who were the other lovers of Fiona that Pauline said she had sent letters to? And the Metropolitan Police, what would they make of all this? And who had been her first caller, the one the nurse chased out?

It was too much for my tired brain to handle today. I would confront Will tomorrow. The only good thing that was happening was that Brack was coming to the flat tonight and we could be together again. I could ask him about Pauline's letter to him and find out what she had written to these men. Pauline, I thought, you have managed to almost sabotage my big media launch, claiming to be poisoned and you've accused several men of murder. What more damage can you do!

It turned out to be a lot, lot more.

Chapter 16

I walked back to the flat slowly, my mind awash with too many images, showered and dressed and waited for Brack to show up. I didn't dare take on any more alcohol, so I swigged down a Diet Coke while I dried my hair. I was glad I hadn't told anybody—not a soul—about those nasty notes that Pauline and Fiona had sent so I wouldn't have to tell anyone in the office about her part in them. I somehow sensed John Bowen would not have been as forgiving as I was, and I just hoped Will hadn't blabbed to him.

When Brack appeared, I held on to him, hugging until I finally felt that I might now possibly survive the day and night. I guess all that drama in the hospital had gotten to me. He was free with his compliments about the media launch and I basked in them. I gave him a drink and curled up on the couch next to him. I told him what the doctor had said about Pauline's sickness, but I wasn't really up to telling him everything that she had blurted out to me. Not yet. I wanted to think it all over before I talked to Pauline again. How did I know she was telling the truth in anything?

Yet, somehow, I couldn't stop myself from asking, "Why did she say to you, 'Was it you? Did you try to shut me up?' when we were trying to get her to the car?"

He shook his head. "I haven't a clue. Remember, she got

at Will, too, before she collapsed. Woman was daft, you know, thinking she was poisoned. Let's forget Pauline and go on with our own life."

He emptied his glass, pulled me up from the sofa, kissed me lightly and put on his jacket. "No more Pauline talk, no more shop talk. It was a great launch, so now we can both relax. I've been away so much these past weeks that I need to get back to my flat before we have dinner. Coming with me?"

You bet I was, so off we went to his flat and went right to bed. It had been a long two weeks alone. We both dozed off afterwards, but when we woke it was still light—those long London twilights in June are incredible—and so we strolled to a pub for a drink and a sandwich. No more rich food, with or without Sweet Whippo, we both agreed. It was a glorious English evening, so we walked down to Gentlemen's Row, a group of houses set by a stream, and stood on the bridge looking down at the slow-moving, slightly greenish water. We barely said anything to each other, content to be together. We strolled some more. The village was still full of people walking dogs or sitting on benches. I was absolutely, perfectly content.

It was heaven to fall into bed again, knowing that the dreaded day was over, Pauline was recovering and Brack was back in town. (Pay no attention to the image of the cold, stuffy Englishman in bed—that's a canard put out by the French.) In the very early morning, I opened my eyes to see Brack standing at one side of the bedroom window, looking out. I stretched and sat up in bed, and he turned around and smiled at me.

"What time is it?" I asked.

"Half after the hour."

"What hour?"

"Four."

"Then come back to bed."

"In a minute. I was just going over some things in my mind."

"What things?"

"Will's actions."

I sat up straight, my brain beginning to come back to life.

"What do you mean, Will's actions?"

"You'll find out all about it tomorrow—today, I mean," he said. "I told John Bowen the details this afternoon at the luncheon. I took Will off after our hospital visit and put it to him."

"Find out what?"

"Are you sure you can take it? You've had a rough day."

"Tell me, tell me."

"It's bloody astonishing. Well, for starters, Will has been working behind my back with another company, a company that plans to bring out a competing product to Sweet Whippo soon. That's why he tried to delay this launch and that's why I had the party brought forward. Now, of course, Will's for the chop. John will see to that today."

I sat back, stunned. Here I had thought Will had been trying to get at me, wanting to make me look nonprofessional, resenting my American presence, yet all along he had been busy sabotaging Sweet Whippo for his own benefit or for the benefit of this other company. Was the name S&C? That had been the name of the company mentioned in Fiona's pilfered papers.

"I couldn't tell you before I told John," he went on, "and of course I didn't want to worry you. You had enough on your plate just getting through the launch, and I certainly hadn't anticipated Pauline's scene. And to be selfish, I wanted you to myself for a while, without shop talk. It was worth it, wasn't it?"

"This is incredible!" I sat straight up again. "How did you find out?"

He didn't answer.

"I mean, who spilled the beans?"

He still didn't say anything.

Suddenly I knew. It had been Fiona. That's what all the drafts of those letters I had found in her flat had been about. Could she have been working for Will and his new company already? The company had to be the S&C mentioned in those papers. Or had she double-crossed Will by telling Brack about Will's defection just before she died? Whose side was she really on?

Brack started walking toward the bed.

"I'll bet Fiona knew all about it!" I blurted out.

He stopped, just a few feet away, obviously startled.

"Why do you say that? Tell me, why did you say that?" he persisted.

"Oh, I don't know," I stammered. "She and Will were close, and she kept acting like she knew something I didn't know. Or maybe I'm just being paranoid about the British again."

He sat down on the side of the bed, looked hard at me, then shrugged and slipped in under the covers.

"Forget about Fiona and forget that I said anything about Will. John will explain it all tomorrow, but that's why I've been on the Continent, tracking down the facts. Now it's up to your agency to take action. Put Fiona out of your mind. I promise you everything will be much, much better now for you."

I opened my mouth to ask more questions, but he leaned over, covered my mouth with his, his hands reached for me and I forgot what I was going to say. I told myself I would talk everything over with him first thing in the morning, and I could ask whether Pauline was telling the truth when she said she had sent him an accusing letter.

I slept heavily, and when I awoke, the sun was streaming in the window and the other side of the big bed was empty. There was a note lying there on the crumpled sheet, a note telling me that he had to leave early, sorry, please make sure the door was locked on my way out and he would see me today at MWBV's offices.

And, oh yes, it had been a really rave night.

By the time I got dressed, took a train and taxi back to my own flat, showered and chose an outfit for the office, I was running two hours late. I called Jane with my excuses, biting my tongue to keep from blurting out the news about Will, merely telling her I was off to pick up Pauline. I looked up the hospital's telephone number, finally got through to them and talked to some very helpful person who told me I didn't need to come to escort Miss Greene.

"A young American, very nice he was, collected her just a few minutes ago. A chef, he told me while he was waiting, over here to do a contest, actually a colleague of Miss Greene's. Ever so helpful. And there was yet another chef with him, a man I've seen on the telly many times."

Robert and Nigel. What was going on here?

Just as I reached for the telephone again to call Jane and ask for Pauline's home address—there was no way I was going to leave that woman alone with Robert and Nigel and have her tell them all the weird stuff she had told me—the instrument rang, making me jump. It was Jane herself and her voice squeaked with excitement.

"Lucille, thank God you're still there. Listen, Mr. Evans Jones, our world leader, the great man himself, has been looking for you. So has John Bowen and so has Braxton Clark. They all three came into this office and asked for you, in person. They want you right away in John's office for a big meeting. I didn't like the look on Jones' face. Grim. What have you done? Tell me, tell me."

"Don't worry, Jane, I think I know what's it's all about. Tell them I'll be there in five minutes, ten minutes at the most."

I made it in five, straight to John's office, past his guardian secretary with just a nod. Our agency's worldwide leader was there and he did indeed look grim. John had on his "everything is jolly, not to worry" face, but Brack looked serious and during the usual hellos and seating arrangements, he managed to mutter to me, "Don't forget to act surprised."

"Sit down, Miss Anderson, and listen carefully, please," said Evans Jones. He was a big bear of a man, overflowing the armchair behind John's desk as he leaned back, fingers steepled on his chest. He had long, straight silver hair and eyes so dark they seemed black. Those eyes were focused on me as I sat down.

"It has come to our attention that we have a traitor in our midst," he said, shaking his head in amazement.

He was really putting it strong, but I didn't move a muscle.

"Will Hammersmith has been dealing with the enemy."

God, he made it sound like the KGB was at work. I kept looking straight at him, allowing shock to register.

"All the while he was leading the campaign for Sweet Whippo, he was working behind our backs for a competing company."

I let my mouth drop open and made a little noise of disbelief.

"Yes, our Will has let the side down."

Now we were into game clichés. I opened my mouth to ask suitable questions, but he held up one big hand and shook his head.

"Here's what we are going to do. First, of course, our Will gets the chop. In fact, he has already been dismissed and his secretary is standing guard so there will be no removal of any files. He will be sent the carton of his personal belongings, of course."

I was sure Will had long ago cleaned out and taken home all the pertinent files, but I nodded approval.

"The campaign will go on as planned for Sweet Whippo because I feel that Will will not be able to deflect our progress, even now. I am sorry I was not in town yesterday because I heard you did a perfectly splendid job with the launch."

I smiled modestly and murmured my thanks, saying it had been a joint effort, of course.

"Now I want you to consider taking over the stewardship of the account. Is that agreeable with you?"

Agreeable! At last I could really operate.

"Yes, of course," I said. "I consider it a privilege and I do have a wonderful staff. I must admit I am stunned by Will's actions. I never suspected anything." That part was true.

"Neither did we. No one here twigged to the situation." He turned and glared at John. "Braxton Clark, our client, had to track the facts down."

I turned and looked at Brack, but his face stayed solemn. John started huffing and puffing and saying something about this had never happened before, not with his people, don't you know. We all knew he was lying. Things like this had happened before far too often, as they did in any advertising agency.

"Now," Evans Jones said, heaving his bulk from the chair and leaning forward, "we must all agree on what we will tell our agency people, not to mention any snoopers from the media. We will put out a release saying because of the success of yesterday's launch, we are intensifying the American thrust and you will be handling the campaign directly. Will Hammersmith will be pursuing other interests. Sound right to you, Clark?"

Typical corporate talk, I knew, but hey, I was now in charge! No more Will to bug me. I tried not to grin, and instead kept on my sincere look. Evans then asked what was my next step in the campaign and I burbled on enough to keep him happy. "By the way," I said, offhand, very offhand. "What is the name of this company that Will was involved with?"

I held my breath, but when the words "S&C" came forth from John's lips, I had to stifle any comment and just shook my head in disbelief. I still hadn't told anyone about those papers of Fiona's still resting in my flat. I wouldn't need to, now. When the meeting broke up, Brack said goodbye pleasantly, told me he would be in close touch, and he and Evans Jones went off together, with John trotting right behind, in charge of seeing to the release of this news.

As soon as I got back to my office and opened the door, I knew that the grapevine had already been at work. I said to the assembled PR staff, "What have you heard?"

"Will's been sacked, that's what we heard," Jane answered. "Is it true? Out on his ear, only one step ahead of the dreaded security people. What did he do?"

"You bet it's true," I answered. "What he did was to go to work, undercover of course, for another firm that has a similar product to Sweet Whippo, so he could sabotage Whippo, particularly messing up our launch, and then calmly introduce his new product. How's that for company loyalty!"

"A mole, a real mole," said our secretary.

"A real shit, I'd call him," Jane said. "How did they find out?"

"I'm not really sure," I admitted, "but the good news is that I'm the new account supervisor on Sweet Whippo, as of right now, and we have been given permission to go on to greater glory."

"Super," said Jane. "What happens to Will now?"

"Probably be hired by the other company, something called S&C. I'll probably find out tonight from Braxton Clark."

I didn't miss the look that flew between Jane and our secretary.

"In the meantime, we all have a lot of follow-up work to do, so let's get on with it. We've got to take this show on the road and open in Bristol in a week. At least, that's what we originally planned. Can you get to Gillian and see if Will left any notes about the ad side of the campaign? I'll find out from John who will be taking his place."

Jane walked to the door and looked back for a moment before grinning at me and giving me the thumbs-up sign.

I got Pauline's home number and address from the personnel office and telephoned her. When she recognized my voice, she started in apologizing again, telling me that she had only done this once before in her life, and she had no idea that those pills, the ones the doctor had given her for her nerves, were so powerful. I broke into this recital.

"Pauline, I'll be right over to see you. I think we need to have a little talk."

She gasped and stuttered, "No, no, I'm perfectly fine. Please don't bother."

"I insist. Be there in a jiffy." I hung up before she could say anything more.

I dashed outside and of course had trouble finding a cab. It took just under five minutes to get to her flat, but I spent another few minutes buzzing her intercom, trying to get her to answer her bell. What was she doing? She knew I was on my way over. When she finally buzzed me in, I climbed up three flights of stairs to meet her standing in her doorway, clad in a silky dark blue robe. She looked much, much better, her skin not so pale, her eyes not puffy. She led me into the sitting room and offered me the sofa as she seated herself on a straight-back chair. She gave me a frightened look, and I wondered if she thought I was here to bawl her out. There was no sign of Robert or Nigel.

"Are you sure you shouldn't be in bed, Pauline?"

She looked at a closed door, which I assumed led into her bedroom.

"No, no," she said, her voice weak. "I'm feeling much better. It's just that the bedroom is in such a mess. I'd rather talk here."

I shrugged and settled back on the sofa. Pauline remained perched primly on her chair.

"It was nice of Robert and Nigel to pick you up at the hospital and bring you here. I was going to do it, you know."

She didn't say anything, just stared straight at me, those blue eyes wide.

"Pauline, have you told anyone about the notes you sent to me and about those letters you sent to those men?"

"No, no, I haven't, really I haven't, Lucille. I'm so

ashamed." She hung her head and picked at the folds of her elegant silk robe. I noticed now that she had on mascara, powder and lipstick. Had that been for the ride home with my two chefs?

"You haven't said anything to anyone about Fiona's part in sending those nasty notes, have you?" I asked.

Her indrawn breath was answer enough, but she shook her head firmly. "I don't want to sully her memory. I told you she only sent one. I sent the others, I'm ashamed to say. Very, very sorry."

When I told her the news about Will Hammersmith, she made a slight noise and her blue eyes opened wide, and she cast another quick look at the bedroom door. Was someone in there? I felt this desire to get up and fling that door open, but didn't have the nerve. She swayed a little, then sat up, making an obvious effort to stay upright.

"Pauline, are you all right? Here, you must lie down." I got up from the sofa and took her hand, a cold clammy hand, and pulled her toward the sofa. She followed and lay down, heaving a sigh, while I stuffed a couple of pillows behind her head. Then she closed her eyes.

Without opening them she said in a small voice, "Poor Will Hammersmith. What a pity. I feel even worse about my little fit and then telling you he must have put some stuff on the puddings. Oh God, I am deeply ashamed about my fears. I don't know what came over me."

I wanted to say, about a ton of tranquilizers and booze came over you, but I shut my lips firmly.

"Fiona loved him, you know," her voice went on, stronger now. "He loved her, too, she told me. She knew he did, but he didn't tell anybody. I think they were going to get married after . . ." Her voice trailed off.

"After what, Pauline?"

There was a long silence.

"Pauline?"

"I don't think I should talk about it," she said softly.

"About what?" She had a dreamy expression on her face and I wondered if she had taken another tranquilizer.

"Nothing, nothing. I could tell that something exciting was going to happen, but I didn't know what, and Fiona said everything would work out and she would have a better job and so would I. It had something to do with Will, but she wouldn't tell me. She said she had some cleanup to do, first, to get rid of somebody."

Those words came tumbling out. Pauline sat up suddenly, looked straight at me, her eyes blazing.

"That's why she sent the first note, because she said she didn't want you to mess things up, because it was tricky and you didn't know how to handle it, being American. I knew it had something to do with Sweet Whippo because she said that Mr. Clark was coming over that night."

"But he didn't go, you know." Actually, I didn't know if that was true or not, but I had to defend Brack. "Will and Fiona were in this together, you better think about that! But what I need to know is did you really send letters to him and three other men you suspect of killing Fiona? Your little list."

She winced when I said that so coldly, but looked me straight in the eye and asked, "What list?"

"The list you told me about yesterday in the hospital. You said you had written letters to four of Fiona's lovers, including Braxton Clark, and said they had to prove to the police that they weren't there that night. You said you sent a copy of the letter to Inspector Reid, that man who did the investigation of Fiona's death."

"Lucille, I can't remember all the things I said in the

hospital. I was so sick." She looked at the bedroom door again.

"But I remember. I think you should call Reid and discuss it with him. Now. Before any more trouble happens. Tell him what you did."

She lay back and closed her eyes. "I don't want to talk any more, Lucille. I will not say another word. You must go, now!" She pushed me so hard I almost fell off the sofa. "Get out! Please. Just leave me alone. Go away. Please. Now, before anything happens!"

Chapter 17

What did she mean, "before anything happens?" I didn't like hearing that. But I gave up and said, "Okay, Pauline, you are obviously tired and I need to get back to the office and finish up some things. Call me if you need anything and I'll send someone over. Perhaps Robert."

She turned her head away. I looked at the bedroom door and dared myself to go over to it, but she turned and looked at me then and I could see something in her eyes. Was it fear? I got up and, avoiding even looking at the bedroom door, I said loudly, "Goodbye, Pauline, you'd better go back to bed and rest." I walked toward the front door of the flat, turned to look at her again to discover she was watching me closely. I took a quick look into the small kitchen just off the living room, but there was no one in there. I spotted a pile of white clothing piled on a stool. I stepped closer to look at it and identified a white chef's jacket. I didn't think it would be Pauline's, as I'd always seen her wearing a dark blue smock or a bib apron in the test kitchens. I wanted to go in that kitchen and look at the jacket, but when I glanced back, Pauline was now getting up from the sofa, eyes focused on me. I gave a little goodbye wave of my hand. She must have sensed that I planned to leave her front door open just a crack so I could see if someone would come out of the bedroom, because she followed me to the door, silk robe billowing behind her. Without another word, not even a goodbye, she shut the door behind me with a definite slam.

I stood for a moment outside on the landing, right up against the door, but strain as I did, I couldn't hear any voices.

Lucille, I said to myself on the way back to the office, you are letting your imagination run away with you, yet the jacket on that stool was definitely a professional chef's jacket. Could it be Robert's or even Nigel's, left there after they brought her home from the hospital? Perhaps one of them was still there and might have been too embarrassed to come out when they heard my voice. Even so, it's no business of yours if Pauline has a friend stashed away in the bedroom, chef or no chef, and for all you knew Pauline could have a steady boyfriend she didn't want you to see. But then, why did she look so fearful? Lucille, give up on Pauline for today. You are tired, you need to calm down. Think about the good news. You are the new account supervisor, you can run things now. You've got a great staff, great chefs and a great client. I smiled, thinking about that client and what would happen during our time together tonight. I could even ask Brack myself if he had been at Fiona's flat that evening and I could also ask him whether he'd gotten one of Pauline's accusing letters. I would be subtle in my interrogation, but at least it would put my mind at rest. But suppose he said, yes, he was there and, yes, he'd got a letter. What would my next step be? Brack was right. It's time for me to give up my detective career and get back to work. Let Pauline just do her own thing. She seemed to have forgotten all about asking me to help her find out about Fiona's death. Something else is going on, though, and she was definitely frightened. But what could I do?

The office seemed unusually quiet for a Thursday afternoon, but Jane assured me everyone was busy pulling the next media presentation together. Robert was nowhere to be seen and when I asked about him, Jane frowned.

"I think he dashed off before you did, said he had some things to buy. Haven't seen him since."

Could that have been Robert in the bedroom? Pauline and Robert? It wasn't impossible. But would Pauline have that look of fear in her eyes because of Robert? I didn't think so. I shook off any more such thoughts and spent the rest of the afternoon shuffling papers and topping it off with a boastful telephone call to Barry Boyle in New York Office, telling him about Will Hammersmith, the media intro, dropping the name of Evans Jones, bragging that I was now in charge. Barry let me rattle on and then gently told me that he had been consulted by Evans Jones and John Bowen last night and had of course assured them I could handle the account.

I should have known.

Another blow occurred late in the afternoon when I got a telephone call from Brack's secretary regretting that a change in plans meant he would not be calling round tonight, but it was definitely on for tomorrow night. Why couldn't he have called me himself, I muttered as I put the phone down.

At that moment it rang again. It was Robert and he was talking so fast I couldn't understand him.

"Slow down, Robert. What is it you are trying to tell me?"

"I'm trying to tell you that Pauline isn't in her flat. I

took over this whole dinner I had just made for her but I rang and rang her bell and she didn't answer. Do you know where she is?"

"Why would I know?"

"Because Jane said you had gone to see her this afternoon and she might have told you where she was going. I got really worried and finally buzzed the landlady, the one that lives downstairs, to go up and open her door. I told her that Pauline had just got out of the hospital and could be lying unconscious upstairs, so she took a key and we went up there together but when we went inside, Pauline was not there."

"She was certainly there when I left, Robert. Maybe she went out for some air, maybe a short walk."

"No, I had just talked to her maybe ten minutes before I got here, to tell her I was coming right over with her food and she said she thought she'd go back to bed because she was feeling worse. She told me not to come, but I knew she needed a good meal."

I started to say something, but he interrupted me. "Listen, Lucille, please listen." He was talking even faster now, the words tumbling out. "When we went into the bedroom, her robe and nightgown were on the bed, so she must have dressed and gone out. There was a torn-off piece of paper lying on top of the robe with a couple of words on it. It said, 'Must tell Lucille.' Just those three words. 'Must tell Lucille.' Tell you what, Lucille?"

It took a while but I finally calmed Robert down by asking him to stay put in Pauline's flat to wait for her return. "I haven't the faintest idea what she means about telling me something. She probably just wrote a note to remind herself of something and then went out to run an errand." I was worried, though.

He agreed, reluctantly, to wait a few more minutes for her return and I turned back to my work, but it was less than five minutes before he was on the telephone again.

"I called Nigel to see if he knew where she was, but Paul said Nigel was doing a shoot somewhere all afternoon. Lucille, I'm really, really worried."

I gave up and said I'd join him at Pauline's flat and we'd think of something. I remembered the chef's jacket I'd seen draped over the stool in Pauline's kitchen. What did I really know about Pauline's personal life anyway? Was there really something going on between Robert and her? But surely she couldn't be afraid of good old Robert.

The taxi deposited me at Pauline's building and Robert buzzed me into Pauline's flat and showed me the slip of paper with the words, "Must tell Lucille." I wanted to think it was harmless, but it was written in large letters with a green felt-tipped pen, almost a scrawl. I remembered Pauline's writing on recipes as small and precise. Robert, talking away, followed me into the kitchen. The white jacket was gone. A big plastic bag with Selfridge's Food Halls logo on the side—Robert's meal offerings—was sitting on that stool. Aside from a glass on the counter in front of the ordinary canisters of flour, tea, coffee and sugar, the kitchen gave me no clues. Oh yes, there were a couple of small bottles of pills with chemist's labels on them, but they were smeared so that I couldn't read them. They could have been anything from aspirin to opium. I went into the small bedroom, where a single bed was unmade, a duvet hanging half onto the floor and the nightgown and robe draped across it. I could see no sign of a recent visitor, yet I could almost feel a presence, and I still thought there had been someone in this bedroom listening to that conversation between Pauline and me. Robert watched me from the bedroom door as I opened the small closet and looked at Pauline's clothes.

"What are you looking for, Lucille?"

"I haven't the faintest idea, Robert, but I don't know what else to do. Tell me, have you and Pauline been seeing each other, I mean besides work?"

"Is that wrong?" he asked, immediately on the defensive.

"Of course not," I stammered. "I just didn't realize. Do you know if she saw other men?"

"Why are you asking these questions now, Lucille?"

"Because I thought she might have gone off with somebody, somebody who came by after I left." Should I ask him about the chef's jacket and Pauline's evasive actions?

Robert pondered a bit and then said, "I do think Pauline might have been seeing someone, because she hinted at it. We weren't serious, you know, but we did spend a lot of time together."

"A chef?" I asked casually, flipping through the hangers in Pauline's closet.

"What do you mean a chef? Oh, you mean was she seeing a chef? Why a chef? You're not making sense, Lucille." No, that wasn't his jacket.

"I don't know what I mean. For instance, she and Nigel seemed to know each other pretty well. Perhaps he was part of her life."

Robert laughed. "That'll be the day. Nigel said she got on his nerves. He wasn't very kind when he talked about her, told me he had worked with her before, but you know, Lucille, London is a real small town when it comes to the foodies, and I've heard some nasty comments about a lot of people I don't even know."

I gave up, went back into the small sitting room and sat down on the sofa. I really wanted out of the flat, out of this situation. I was convinced that Pauline had got dressed and gone off with somebody, that somebody who had been in her bedroom, but Robert seemed so troubled that I hated to leave him alone to wait for Pauline's return. So there we sat, Robert staring down at his feet, the note to me still held in his hand. Pauline's flat was small, but I could see signs that she had tried to make it as elegant as Fiona's. She had even chosen the same peach colored fabric for the sofa and matching chair that I remembered from Fiona's place. There were piles of food magazines stacked on the coffee table, and I picked up an issue of BBC's *Good Food* magazine and started idly leafing through its beautiful color pages of food and personalities. When I turned a page and saw a photograph of Fiona with a panel of TV chefs, it started me thinking. Could Pauline have gone over to Fiona's flat? But why? True, she probably was dutifully checking on it, or maybe she went over to look for something. Something specific. I looked up at Robert's anxious face and decided to go into action.

"You know, Robert, I have a hunch where Pauline might be. I'll bet you she went over to Fiona's flat. She has a key and she might well have decided to go do some more clearing out. She told me that Fiona's mother had been ill and had not been down to tend to the flat and so she was still keeping an eye on it. Let's go over there." At least it would get us out of this depressing flat.

Robert, ever the practical one, said, "Why don't you call from here first?"

"Good idea." I found a telephone directory in the desk drawer and looked up Fiona's number. When I dialed it, I got a busy or "engaged" signal. I waited a few moments, then I called it again, and it was still busy.

"See," I said, "she's over there talking on the phone.

166

Let's go. It's worth a try. I went to Fiona's flat with Pauline once, but I can't remember exactly where it was. I do seem to remember that Pauline said Fiona's flat was near hers." I wrote down the address from the directory and stood up.

Robert's anxious face cleared a little and he got up and went into the kitchen to take foil-wrapped packages out of his bag of food and carefully store them away in the small fridge. Together we walked out the door, making sure it locked behind us. We stopped at the landlady's flat downstairs and Robert thanked her again for letting him inside the flat. She gave us a very suspicious look, but made no comment except to say that she would of course tell Ms. Greene that she had let us in because it seemed such an emergency. I read off Fiona's address and she told us it was just a couple of blocks away. Her face said that she thought she had made a mistake in letting us in, so we escaped before any more comments came forth. I was happy to get out of Pauline's flat, as sensing Robert's anxiety, yet not wanting to tell him about my conversation with Pauline and my suspicions about someone in her bedroom, had left me with a feeling that something was dreadfully wrong.

Chapter 18

Robert kept asking me questions about Pauline's personal life as we walked the few blocks, following the landlady's directions. These were questions I couldn't answer. I didn't really know anything about Pauline, except that she had given me nothing but trouble and I knew that Robert wouldn't want to hear my complaints. I wondered again just how involved he was with her. Could that white jacket have been his and he didn't want to admit it? I was relieved when I recognized the building where Fiona's flat was, so I pointed it out and he made a beeline for the door and the buzzer system, turning to ask me, "Is F. Gordon the name we want?" When I nodded, he buzzed, waited, then buzzed again. When there was no answer, he pushed the bell with all his might and held it there. Still no response. He turned to me, asking, "If she's there, why doesn't she answer?"

I shrugged. "Maybe she's still on the phone."

But he wouldn't accept that, and pushed the buzzer again. No response. I moved him aside gently, looked at the names on the bells and saw "Tate."

"That's the name of the woman who lives on the ground floor. Let's see if she'll let us in the front door at least. Fiona's flat is one flight up," I said, pushing the little gold bell beside her name.

We both jumped when a voice barked out at us, "Who is it?"

I explained who I was and what we were doing there and how worried we were about Pauline and could she please just let us in the front door. There was a long wait and then a buzzer sounded. We grabbed the door and pushed ourselves in. Mrs. Tate's flat door was slightly ajar, a chain firmly across it. I went over there and introduced myself again to the stony face behind the chain, reminding her that I had been here with Pauline Greene after Fiona Gordon's death. Robert had already gone up the stairs, two at a time. When Mrs. Tate finally nodded and shut her door, I walked upstairs myself. I could never look at those steps without visualizing Fiona tumbling down them. Robert was standing at the top of the flight, impatiently waiting for me.

"Is this her flat? Look, the door's open," he said, pointing to it. It was indeed slightly ajar. Then he slowly pushed it in and we peered around. No one in the drawing room. We looked at each other and he walked in and I followed. The elegant flat looked much the same to me, if a little dusty.

"Pauline?" he said loudly. "Are you here?"

No answer. I stepped in front of him and went straight to the bedroom, opening the closed door firmly. I stopped so suddenly at what I saw that Robert crashed into me from behind. There in Fiona's big double bed lay Pauline, covers up to her chin, asleep!

Robert looked stunned, but walked over to the side of the bed and leaned down over her. "Pauline, Pauline, wake up," he said gently. Then when she didn't move, he asked, "Pauline, are you all right?" Obviously worried, he took her face in his hands and turned it toward him, then dropped one hand to her shoulder, shaking her very gently. Her eyes didn't open. He turned to me and said, "She's drugged. She's in a coma."

Not drugs again, I thought. I went around to the other side of the bed and pulled down the covers. She was fully dressed in slacks and shirt and shoes. I looked at her face again and touched her cheek. That face was ice cold. My hand started shaking. Maybe she wasn't in a coma. Maybe it was worse.

"Call 999, Robert. She looks pretty bad; let's get her to the hospital." Our eyes met across the bed. He shook his head in disbelief. Coma or worse, I did know something had to be done right away.

"Dial 999," I repeated, and we both looked around for the telephone. I saw it first, lying on the floor, receiver off the cradle—the reason for the busy signal. I picked it up, put it back, listened for the dial tone and then slowly punched in 999. When the voice asked me which service, I hesitated, then said, "Ambulance" and went through the procedure of giving them the address and telephone number. Before they could disconnect, I said, "Maybe you'd better send the police, too," and hung up. I looked around at Robert, who was still hovering over Pauline, trying to get her awake. Then I saw the small bottle of pills lying on the floor, half hidden by the bedspread. I started to pick it up, then remembered I probably shouldn't touch anything, so left it there. I warned Robert not to touch it. At least I was following proper police procedure gleaned from all those mysteries I had read.

The next few hours were a blur. First, the ambulance crew came and worked with Pauline, gently pushing Robert aside. He had been holding Pauline's hand. We stood there, watching them trying to revive her and I told them in a slightly shaky voice that she might have taken some prescription drugs; they asked us questions about what kind of drugs. All I could do was point at the bottle of pills. They picked up the bottle, read the label, and worked on Pauline some more. The police showed up and there were more questions, but when the ambulance crew turned around and left without Pauline, I knew the news was bad. Nobody would tell us anything, just asked us to wait, please. A police ambulance crew then showed up and they put Pauline's body on a gurney and carried her down the stairs. Both Robert and I started to follow them, God knows why, but a man in plain clothes stopped us and politely but firmly told us to follow him into the sitting room. Robert gave one last pitiful glance at the sad procession.

The man introduced himself as Detective Inspector Johnston Reid, and made us sit down in Fiona's drawing room. Gently, he said, "I'm very much afraid this woman is dead. Very sorry. I shall have to ask you questions."

He waited for us to get over the shock of hearing that statement, but politely deflected our questions. We took turns identifying ourselves and telling him why we were here and the quizzing, all very polite, continued. I explained who Pauline was and why she was in this flat, and I blurted out the tale about Fiona and her death just a few weeks ago. I went through it all, telling the story and trying to explain about Pauline and why the flat was still not cleared out because of Fiona's mother's illness. I think I began to babble. Inspector Reid was kind enough to stop me and tell me that he knew all about that case as he had been involved in it. I started asking him questions, but he turned them all aside. Then Robert kept saying over and over he had to go to Pauline, but we were told her relations had to be notified first and brought forth. Inspector Reid asked me where Pauline lived and when I told him just a few blocks away, he got up, talked to a couple of uniformed men, left them there and asked us to go with him in his car to Pauline's flat, where he knocked on the door of the long-suffering landlady, got the keys from her with no questions and shepherded us up-stairs. He found a list of names by her telephone, but nei-ther Robert nor I knew which were relatives. I told them to call MWVB Personnel Department, but of course it was al-ready too late and the office was closed. It went on like this until I complained, almost in tears, that I was too tired to think. Finally, after notifying us we had to show up at head-quarters the next morning at ten a.m. for yet another ses-sion of questioning, Inspector Reid told us to go.

"Scotland Yard?" I asked, and then was immediately ashamed of myself. Admit it, Lucille, you've always wanted to see that place, but this is callous of you. I put it down to shock.

Inspector Reid shook his head and gave us a card with his name and the location of the police station handling this area and told us to go home and get some sleep. He prom-ised he would answer my questions tomorrow.

In the cab on the way home, Robert wanted to keep talking about Pauline, but I was so bushed and in shock and told him I simply could not utter another word. It had been a nightmare and I still couldn't believe that Pauline was gone. I dropped him off at his hotel and I went on and got myself up to my flat. I telephoned Jane and left a message on her machine, telling her what had happened, and would she please again notify the necessary people and I would be in tomorrow as usual. I put the mute on the phone, turned down the volume on the answering machine, undressed and fell into bed. Of course, I couldn't sleep. I lay there with thoughts chasing each other through my mind. Why had she done it? Or had someone given her the pills or made her take them? Why was she in Fiona's flat? Why was the door unlocked? Was she waiting for someone? Had she gone there to meet someone? Who? These thoughts went round and round in my head as I finally gave up and took a sleeping pill. Anything to shut up that voice in my head.

When I awoke around nine-thirty the next morning after troubled and restless hours of sleep, where in spite of the pill Pauline's face had floated in and out of my dreams, I forced myself to listen to the messages on the machine. Jane had rung back frantically, and Robert had been on it earlier. I got through to Jane at the office and told her more about the situation. After a moment of stunned silence and appropriate words, she told me she had already notified various people, including the Personnel Department and they were waiting for me to get there. I explained that first we had to go to the police station.

"Do you want the company's lawyers to go with you?" Jane asked.

"We're not charged with murder, Jane," I snapped, "not even 'helping the police with their enquiries,' " which in England means under suspicion. "We're just answering questions."

"Sounds serious to me," said Jane, "but I'll be here if you need lawyers."

I got hold of Robert, who was barely articulate, and I told him I would pick him up. A taxi ride took us to the address on Inspector Reid's card, and the police station disappointingly turned out to be a small, nondescript modern building. Robert and I went through all the reception preliminaries and were finally escorted, "Visitor" badges and all, to the office of Detective Inspector Reid. His office was furnished in tacky modern with a scarred desk and plastic chairs. I told myself that he was definitely not Inspector Morse, but doing his best. Why do these detective story thoughts constantly take over my mind? I should be feeling desolate for Pauline. He finally told us that Pauline was in the morgue awaiting identification by her sister and no, we could not go see her. This was Robert's request, not mine. There was no way I was going into any morgue. We answered more questions, but he carefully deflected my questions, promising again that he would talk to me later about Pauline's and Fiona's deaths. He thanked us, handed me another card, said I should ring him if I thought of anything he should know, but otherwise he would be in touch with me and sent us on our way. So much for grilling by the Metropolitan police. Admit it, Lucille, part of you is busy filing all this away for your murder mystery. You *are* callous.

The office was a madhouse when we got there, with everyone asking questions. Robert fled down into the basement kitchen. I answered what questions I could and then went into my office and shut the door firmly, asking Jane to field the calls. I made a call to Brack and wonder of wonders, he was in his office. I blurted out the whole story and he listened without comment until finally he broke in.

"You need to get away from all this, Lucille. Remember that trip to Henley I promised you? Now is the right time to go. When you finish at the office today, I'll call at your flat, if I may, and we can start the weekend. How does that sound to you?"

It sounded like heaven and that kept me going. When I called Barry Boyle in New York to tell him this latest happening, he said, "You'd better finish up and come home soon, Lucille. London Office sounds full of self-destructive women, falling down stairs and overdosing." I assured him

I wasn't remotely self-destructive and was doing a wonderful job.

I took a deep breath and rang Robert down in the basement kitchen where he told me Pauline's staff had gone into shock over the news and had closed the kitchen down. He finally accepted grudgingly that I wanted to spend a weekend with Braxton, but made it plain that he thought my place was with him and Pauline's sister, recently unearthed from office files. She was coming up to London from Portsmouth. I knew I couldn't handle that.

When Brack appeared at the front door of the flat that evening, he stated, "I'll give you ten minutes to tell me what happened with Pauline and then we won't let her sad death spoil our time." He held up his hand when I started protesting. "I have to admit I never really liked the woman and liked her even less when she almost sank our media launch. A very neurotic woman, I'm afraid. I am sorry about her suicide, though."

So I told him briefly what had happened and he listened carefully. But when I started in on how Pauline had told me that she had sent notes to Fiona's lovers, he flatly refused to answer me when I asked him if he had got that letter that she said she sent him.

"That has nothing to do with you, Lucy. I won't have you doing your amateur detective bit with something that a nutty woman dreamed up. She's ruining our time together. If you don't stop this line of questioning, I'll leave."

I had never seen him so angry. I couldn't bear to think of his leaving, so I shut my mouth. We had drinks at the flat, we went to dinner at his club; now there's a frightening place for an American woman to be, all men and their wives dining in the sedate dining room where women were allowed, many voices, but never above a murmur. I was right in style with my printed dark green silk dress and decorous black jacket and "court shoes"—pumps with medium-height heels. I felt sat upon by all this decorum and I have to admit my conversation was not very sparkling. All I really wanted to do was talk about Pauline and her sad death, but he was adamant. It was not the best of evenings, and even when we went back to my flat and went to bed in that big king-sized bed, there was a coolness between us. He left shortly after midnight and told me he would pick me up the next morning for the drive to Henley.

When Brack was late coming by for me this morning, I figured he was annoyed with me and my persistent questions to him about Fiona and now Pauline, but I was just as angry with him for not wanting to talk to me about it. No matter what excuses I made to myself, it made him look guilty. Of what, I didn't really know. I tried on several outfits and finally settled on black slacks, crisp beige shirt and a red sweater tied carefully around my shoulders and loafers. But he finally showed up, and gave no excuses, but instead complimented me on my outfit. As we took off in his big black car, I couldn't help but remember Mrs. Tate's words about a big black Jaguar parked in front of Fiona's building on that fateful night. The ride was nice because we went on the back roads instead of the motorways so I could see some countryside.

"We're here," he said happily, as he looked for a parking space. I looked around. So this was Henley, the celebrated spot for the annual Royal Regatta, where crews from all over the world rowed their hearts out for school and country. Ever since a former boyfriend of mine had rowed for Kent School and then Harvard, I had heard more about

Henley than I ever really wanted to know. I could see I was
in for more information, as I watched Brack park the car
carefully, and say to me, "Come on, Lucille. Don't
dawdle."

"So this is Henley," I said to Brack as we stood in the
middle of the bridge across the Thames, looking down the
course. "What's so special about it?"

He gave me an exasperated look. "This is just the town
of Henley, and the big event won't take place for about ten
days. See those tents? That's where our firm will have one.
Hospitality Tents, you know, which means free booze and
food, not for the crews, of course, but for our customers
who come to watch. Come on, let's walk down the
towpath."

He was like a child at Christmas, eyes alight, a smile
playing across his face.

"I take it you rowed here once." I almost said, "in your
youth," but bit my tongue in time.

"Yes, for my college at Oxford, actually."

"I'm impressed."

"You should be. We were good. Not good enough,
though, because those enormous American crews often beat
us. You do grow big oarsmen over there."

"Not on Sweet Whippo, that's for sure," I said, taking
his arm in mine. He withdrew it gracefully, beckoning me
on.

"Come on, keep up with me," he ordered. His humor
was better than mine. I was still annoyed that during the
ride here he had again turned away any discussion of my
terrible time with Pauline. "I simply won't talk about it," he
had announced again. I found it hard to join in his happy,
carefree mood. I was sulking.

We walked along the towpath, a long, long walk. Then

we walked back. I was glad I had on loafers, but my feet were beginning to rebel. I hoped I could make it to the place where we'd left the car. When we got back to the bridge, I made it across, then collapsed and sat on the wall at its foot.

"You've earned a pint here," he said, dragging me up and around to the back of the pub, to the outdoor terrace overlooking the river where I sat down gratefully while he went into the bar and came out with two large gins and tonic. "Rest a little, because next we're going to the new River and Rowing Museum. It's new and as I was a contributor to it, I'd like to see what they've done. Heard it was spectacular."

My heart sank at the thought of more walking, but I sighed and began. "Now tell me what's so special about Henley," I asked, after downing most of the drink. I was thirsty and it was actually warm, the sun shining down on us.

"The Regatta, *THE* Royal Regatta," he said patiently. "Crews come from all over the world to compete and this goes on for about a week. So far, the event hasn't been overrun with crowds like Wimbledon because rowing isn't much of a spectator sport. Most of the people who come here were oarsmen once themselves. I mean, where there's time between races, that's when everyone hits the bars. Some bars are limited to members and special guests, and there are a few special places here, like the Leander Club, where everyone wants to go for a drink, but those are limited to members only, so companies like mine set up these hospitality tents for our customers who want to be seen at Henley. Very proper Regatta, this is, and you have to dress correctly for it or you're banished to the outskirts."

"And how will you dress for this oh-so-proper event?"

"In my blazer, white flannels, club tie and cap with club colors, all correct," he said in all seriousness.

I waited for him to say more, something like, "And you'll be dressed properly, too," but there was an awkward silence. So maybe I wasn't going to be invited to this Regatta; maybe I was just brought here to see what the company setup was. Maybe I wasn't considered the right sort for mingling with the upper class sporting crowd. I finished off my drink and handed the glass to him.

He looked at me sharply, but took it and his own and went inside the pub again. I told myself not to get so bitchy, but I felt bitchy. When he returned, I took the glass and took a swig.

"Should we go down and look at your tent?"

"There's nothing there yet."

"So now what do we do?"

"When you finish that, we're going to get in the car and drive to my hosts' place. It's up the river a bit in a great location, right on the river, actually. They've asked me to stay with them during the Regatta. I want to show it to you. Then we'll go to the Museum."

I noticed he had said, "asked me" to stay, nothing about us. Again I felt angry. Why wasn't I going to be part of this big social event? I walked back with him, eyes on the ground, until we got in and then slammed the door hard. He didn't seem to notice. We drove down a winding road for only a mile or so, and then turned into a long, white-graveled drive. The house was impressive. Brack got out of the car and motioned for me to follow him. He didn't go toward the house, but instead went down a path lined with heavy shrubbery. I followed him, a few steps behind. He made a sharp turn to the left and stopped. We were right on the banks of the river, but this wasn't the calm, placid

Thames I had seen from the bridge and on the towpath. This was a whirling, rushing spew of water. He took my arm, pulled me closer to the edge and pointed up the river. I looked and there I saw the reason. There was a lock at the edge of the river across from us and there the Thames was again placid, but near us there was a dam, a weir, holding back part of the water, but letting through the sluice gate a wild rush of tumbling white water, which turned into eddies just inches away. I tried to step back, but he held me firmly right there at the edge.

"How deep is it here?" I asked, looking down into the churning water.

"Deep enough," he answered.

"For what?"

"To throw you in if you don't stop asking questions about Fiona and Pauline's deaths."

I twisted around enough to see his face. Surely this was a joke. But his face was unsmiling as he gazed at me steadily. His grip tightened on me, so much that my arm hurt. I hurt, too, and that hurt slowly turned to anger. How dare he threaten me!

"Why don't you want to answer questions about Fiona and Pauline?" I asked, trying to pull away, but still he held me. "Why can't you tell me? What have you got to hide!" My anger took over my good sense. "What did Fiona really mean to you? I've become very suspicious about you and Fiona being together that night, and Pauline told me she sent a letter to you accusing you and yet you won't talk to me about anything. What do you expect me to think! Why haven't you gone to the police and told them all this? How do I know you didn't push her down those stairs!"

His voice was cold as he asked, "Do you really think I killed Fiona?"

"Why not!" I said, my voice rising in spite of myself. Everything started piling up inside of me, all those unanswered questions. I couldn't seem to stop myself. "Did she tell you about her new job with that company, S&C, did she taunt you about it? Did you lose your temper and slam her down those stairs on your way out? Is that what really happened? No wonder you don't want to hear about Pauline and her evidence. You know, I have some evidence of my own. I've got some of Fiona's papers that I took from her flat." I stopped, aghast at what I had just said.

"What papers?" His voice was angry, too. "What are you talking about? Tell me!"

I twisted around and pulled myself almost free of his grasp, but he was too strong for me.

"Go ahead," I taunted. "Throw me in, if you want, but I still need to know about you and Fiona and Pauline." I must have lost my mind to say this and I started to say I was sorry, but I didn't have a chance.

His grip loosened, his hands dropping down to his sides. It threw me off balance so that I damn near fell in, but I managed to step back from the edge. I tried to turn and walk with dignity but he got hold of me again.

"You damn fool," he said in this cold, cold voice. "You don't know what you're doing, playing this stupid detective game. You're out of your tiny mind. Come on, we're going back to London."

My common sense had come back to me and I also wondered what the hell I was doing, making these accusations to this man, this man I cared so much for, but I couldn't seem to shake off this anger. I pushed his hand away and marched ahead of him down the path, down to the car. "Stay away from me," I ordered. "Take me back to the town and I'll take the train home." I thought that remark would show him how angry I still was.

Without another word, he opened the car door, got in and said, "Get in and I'll do just that." He started the engine and I barely had time to throw myself into the seat before the car took off. Not a word was exchanged between us until he actually drew up in front of the small railroad station.

"Here it is. Help yourself. There's a train about every hour."

I got out, slammed the door and marched over to the platform. I wouldn't let myself look back to see if he were still there watching me. Within a few minutes, I saw a train coming in. It stopped dead at the barriers, I stood back to watch the people get off, and when I spied a man in a conductor's cap, I asked him about the next train.

"It's this one," he said. "It goes back to London in fifteen minutes."

So I got on this small train, which looked more like a streetcar. It was all of two cars long, with no big engine in front. The same conductor came by, took my money, punched me out a ticket, chatted with the other passengers aboard who all seemed to know each other, while I sat, glumly staring out the window, watching the lush countryside, all trees and glimpses of the river gleaming through, as we trundled on to the junction for the fast train to London.

Lucille, Lucille, what have you done!

Chapter 19

When the train rolled into Paddington Station about an hour later, I got off and walked past the barrier into the main part of that bright, noisy, cavernous station, head down, dejected, wondering what to do and where to go now. Why did I have to open my big mouth and play detective again? Just when I thought everything would finally be all right, when Brack and I could be together, when I could find out for sure that he had no real part in Fiona's death so I could put Pauline and her ideas out of my mind, I had to go and mess it up by being so bitchy and stubborn. (Danny had warned me about this particular bad habit months ago and I hadn't listened.)

A blank and dull Saturday afternoon—not to mention Sunday—loomed ahead with no Brack. I then remembered that Robert was looking after Pauline's sister and had wanted me to join them, but I simply could not handle that, not in my present mood. Poor dead Pauline had caused all this trouble between Brack and me, and I was afraid I would take my bitchiness out on her sister. I turned and walked toward the underground station, heading for the flat. Maybe he had called and left a message on my answering machine.

A voice woke me out of my gloom.

"Lucille, Lucille, fancy seeing you here."

It was Will Hammersmith, who had placed himself smack in front of me so that I had to come to a quick stop. He was dressed casually in a light green sports shirt and dark slacks with a white sweater knotted and hanging from his shoulders, fair wavy hair carefully combed, glowing skin with just a light tan, blue eyes clear.

"Hello, Will," I said flatly. We stood looking at each other. "How are you?" was all I could think to add.

"Not too bad," he said. "Going somewhere?" He sounded downright friendly.

No way was I going to tell him that I'd spent the morning quarreling with Brack in Henley.

"Just inquiring about tickets," I lied.

Silence. I stood there, waiting. This was the first time I had seen him since he got thrown out of the London office and I wasn't quite sure what we had to say to each other. He seemed surprisingly cheerful. He looked me up and down and seemed to approve of my outfit, even though my black linen slacks were now rumpled and my crisp beige shirt was no longer crisp. I tugged at my draped sweater and straightened it on my shoulders. I was aware that my once-polished walking shoes had too much of the Henley towpath on them.

"I'm just back from Bath, super place, Bath, and I saw you walking along here, and I said to myself, let bygones be bygones and have a drink with my American nemesis," he said.

"I had nothing to do with your being fired, Will, and you know it."

"You're right. I apologize. In fact, let me give you lunch to show no hard feelings." He smiled winningly at me, all charm.

I was curious about this sudden friendliness, and I was

hungry and I didn't want to go back to an empty flat, so I said, "Why not?" I admit that I was also keenly curious about his involvement with Fiona and S&C and this would be a good time to quiz him. He had disappeared from my life in a sudden puff of smoke since his sins with S&C were found out and I didn't trust this charmer for a minute. God knows what he was up to. But I was nosy enough to hope to find out. Sorry, Brack, but I really can't stop being a detective.

Will took my arm, turned me around and said, "There's a good Indian restaurant just around the corner. It may not sound exciting, but it is a welcome change from continental, not to mention Sweet Whippo."

I shrugged and said, "Sounds good to me. I haven't had any Indian food since I've been here. Lead on." I didn't rise to his comment on Sweet Whippo. I disentangled my arm; he was holding me too tightly, almost painfully so.

We walked through the station and out a side entrance, around the corner, and down the block, making our way through crowds of people doing their Saturday shopping. Abruptly, he grabbed my arm again and steered me down a narrow mews lined with garages, storage buildings and boarded-up shop windows. The street's surface was covered with broken packing crates and rotting fruit and there was not another human being in sight. Will's hand was tight on my arm and a sudden thought rocked me. What was I doing walking down this deserted mews with a man whom Pauline had included in her list of suspects for Fiona's death, a man who had done his best to sabotage me and all my work since my arrival? A man who called me his nemesis? I pulled away quickly and asked, "So where is this Indian restaurant? Not around here, I'll bet. What are we doing in this back alley?"

"Just a short cut," he answered. "Why so jittery?" His

knowing smile at my nervousness made me want to turn and run. "Just there at the turning," he added, pointing to the end of the mews and strode on. I followed a step or two behind, pretending to find something fascinating in the dirty windows of the closed shops we were passing—one filled with empty cardboard cartons and what looked like a dead rat on its back, paws in the air. I shuddered and kept my eyes on Will until we came to the corner. He turned it, looked back at me, and pointed again, smiling. He was enjoying my anxiety. We were back in a busy street, just steps away from the entrance to a restaurant. He ushered me through its doors with a smart bow. It was dark inside, with a heavy aroma of exotic spices and when my eyes became accustomed to the dimness, I saw the ochre-colored walls were covered with garish-colored scenes of India, complete with a giant photo mural of the Taj Mahal at the end. It was definitely not a dim, secluded spot for a tête-à-tête and the place was crowded, so I figured Will couldn't get at me there. Why did I now distrust every man in the U.K., starting with Brack and those swirling waters? I'm getting as batty as poor Pauline.

We were seated at a small table near a front window and a waiter handed us menus the size of a novel. I took one look at it and said, "Pick out something for me, Will. I'm not familiar with Indian food in England. It's probably different from my favorite spot in New York."

He nodded. Both of us were being extremely polite.

When the waiter came back, Will rattled off some selections from the menu, then turned to me and asked, "Is Crab Bengal followed by Lamb Dhansak all right with you?"

I nodded, not wanting to admit I had no idea what either one of those dishes contained, besides crab and lamb.

"Indian beer, too" he said, "highly recommended."

I nodded again. When the waiter departed, we sat there in an uneasy silence. Will was looking down at the table-cloth and I was looking at him, waiting. Finally, he raised his face and leaned across the table, too close. I leaned back.

"I gather my departure was a bit of a shock to you," he began.

"More than a bit. It isn't often I find out that my very own account supervisor is busy working for a rival company at the same time he is giving me orders and instructions."

"It was much more complicated than that," he said, sticking out his chin belligerently. "You see, I was told that Sweet Whippo and S&C were going to merge eventually, so it didn't seem a conflict of interest to me at the time."

I didn't believe a word of this and I let him know by the skeptical look on my face. I even shook my head slightly.

"At any rate, it didn't work out and I got the old heave-ho, so naturally I had to go to work for S&C. Actually, I carried the can for other people, Fiona and Nigel, to name two. Hah, I can see by your face that you didn't know that."

"I knew about Fiona, but I find it hard to believe that Nigel was involved."

"He was a minor player on our team, but how did you know about her?"

I realized I shouldn't have let on about Fiona; no one should know I had stolen those papers from her bedside table in her flat, but I covered myself quickly by saying, "Pauline told me."

He looked closely at me, then shrugged. "Bloody woman always talked too much. But, still, it hasn't turned out too badly, right? You've moved up nicely, everyone thinks you're a marvel and I have a new job with plenty of money and perks."

The waiter showed up with the Indian beer, poured it, departed, and I was spared any more comment until I had taken a hefty swig from my tall glass. It was good, so good that I took a few more swallows, big swallows. On an empty stomach, that was probably a mistake, as I began feeling much better right away. Even though I had failed miserably with Brack, I could also use this lunch to find out if Will had got one of Pauline's accusatory letters. I would show Brack that I could be a detective as well as his current female interest. I looked around the restaurant at the other diners, most of whom seemed in their twenties or early thirties, dressed in jeans and shoes they call "trainers" over here, the same things we call running shoes. This must be their Saturday routine, go to Safeway or Waitrose and then treat themselves to lunch. Some even had their carrier bags of groceries tucked under the tables. Seemed such a normal day, but I looked back at Will with suspicion. What did he really want from me? I knew what I wanted from him, but I waited until the food came, together with another beer, and we had forked in. The crabmeat had been sautéed with onions and tomatoes and spices, not too hot, and Will insisted that I take a bite of his Somosa, a pastry turnover with God knows what mixture inside. Both were delicious, just spicy enough. We were getting very chummy over this food.

The waiter brought more beer and although I knew I should watch my drinking, which always loosens my tongue, I drained my glass and held it out for more. The slight buzz gave me courage to start in on Will.

"Will, we haven't even talked about Pauline's death. That was such a sad thing. I'm sure you heard about it." I knew he still had friends working at MWVB, friends who would keep him up to date on events at the office.

"I'm not at all surprised," he said, "though sorry, of course. The woman had been heading for this for a long time. I heard you and your chef pal discovered her. Grisly, was it?"

"Not nice. Why do you say she was heading for 'this'?" I prompted.

"Remember her ranting at me and at Brack? She was off her nut then," he said. "It wasn't unexpected that she would overdose. She was stuffing those pills down her throat all during the press do, you know, and knocking back glasses of bubbly along with them." He shook his head sadly. "It was bound to happen."

"Did you visit her in the hospital?" I asked. I remembered that the nurse had said that Pauline had had another visitor before I showed up. I also remembered that Pauline had told me she suspected that he had put some stuff on the rice crème that made her sick at the media luncheon. For one anxious moment, it occurred to me that he could do the same here. I pulled my plate closer to me and drank more of the beer. I watched him carefully over the rim of the glass.

"No way I'd go back to that hospital," he answered. "She'd probably have started in on me again. She was hysterical, of course."

"How about when she went home to her flat the next day? Did you stop by?"

He stopped eating and looked hard at me. His eyes were hooded and secretive.

"Why do you ask?"

"Because Pauline talked a lot about you and I think she was a little afraid of you. I thought perhaps you'd gone by to see her after you had been fired."

"Afraid? Nonsense. Why should I visit her? Can't bear the woman." Then he thought a moment and asked, "What exactly did she say about me?"

I calmly went on eating my crab, taking delicate bites. The tension between us grew. I had his complete attention now, but he was too clever to push. He turned in his chair and looked at the people in the big restaurant, murmured, "Always a busy place," then turned and looked back at me. We both waited. I put down my fork, drank still more beer, and started in.

"Among other things, she said you and Fiona were having an affair. She also told me all about those nasty notes I got the first week I arrived, and said you knew about them and approved. Then she said you tried to get her to sabotage our media luncheon by using some sort of stuff that would make people sick. She told me she had sent you a letter saying that she knew you had been at Fiona's flat that evening and you two could have had a lovers' tiff and you knocked her down the stairs." The beer had obviously loosened my tongue and all these accusations rolled out together and in a hurry. I didn't care.

Will stopped eating, wiped his mouth neatly with the napkin and looked coldly at me. "Did you believe that woman's crazy ramblings? No one else did. I was long gone from Fiona's flat before she took that tumble and I can prove it. And what's this about making people sick at the luncheon with some sort of stuff? Why are you nattering on about notes? What notes?"

"Those wonderfully welcoming notes that said, 'Bugger off before something nasty happens.' She told me many more damning things, lying in that hospital bed, thinking she was dying. Quite a lot more. Some about you."

He leaned over the table, his eyes never leaving mine. I

could smell the Indian spices on his breath as he spoke. "I heard you were on this crusade, taking over from Pauline. Why is it you Americans have to be so nosy? Is this a national trait? So we just had a little fun with that first note, a little prank. Pauline then got carried away and sent some more. I warned her to stop."

"That was childish and cruel," I said. "I survived them, but forgive my American nosiness and tell me, did you get a letter from Pauline?"

Before he could answer, the waiter appeared with our main courses, and after they were placed on the table, Will busied himself being host, dishing up the food and commenting on our choice. He was stalling. I watched him as he spooned out my lamb and lentils and I waited until I had his attention before I spoke again.

"Well, did you?"

"Did I what?"

"Did you get a letter from Pauline?"

He took a bite, chewed carefully, then nodded his head in approval of the food before he answered. "I might have. What does it matter?"

"It matters because it proves that Pauline was speaking the truth when she told me she'd sent letters to four men, one of whom was the one who visited her last and killed her."

"Trust Pauline to be dramatic." Then he tilted his head to one side and asked, "Four, eh? Who are the other three?"

"I don't know, but I'm going to find out." I bet he had got the letter. Before I could go on to ask him what had he meant about Nigel being a minor player on the S&C team, he leaned back in his chair and grinned at me.

"Take me off the list, Lucille, dear. I told that detective, what was his name, Reid, where I was at the critical time

191

and he vetted it. I don't know why you don't give up this amateur sleuthing on behalf of the dear girl. The case is closed. You've got enough work to keep you busy until you go back to New York." He smiled another of those charming smiles and added, "Or would you like to stay in London because of Clark? Your hero, Braxton Clark? You could always come work for me if the firm doesn't keep you on." He laughed lightly at his own wit. "Or if Clark strays again—Fiona could have told you about his roving eye—you could consider me. I could learn to like American women, you know. You all have such great legs."

If my mouth hadn't been full, it would have dropped open. As it was, I almost choked before I could get control and wash the food down with beer. Will Hammersmith was actually hitting on me. So that's what he wanted—my great legs and the body attached to them. Still, if I was reading his eye contact correctly, he was serious, quite serious. After the fiasco with Brack this morning, my ego had been battered, but now I felt almost giddy. But what did he mean, "if Clark strays again?"

"You Brits work fast," I said, "but I'm happy with Brack for now. However, you never know. I might consider it my duty to help my fellow American women improve their standing with you. Check with me in a week or so." That shook him a little, which was my aim, but he reached over and grabbed my hand, which was slightly greasy from the fried papadums that I had been crunching. He didn't seem to notice, just squeezed away. We smiled at each other, then I gently freed my hand and wiped it on a napkin.

"What's for afters?" I asked, calmly.

"We could always have that at my place," he said.

"Not very subtle and not today," I said. "I've got more work to do on Pauline's crusade." That cooled him off. I was still suspicious of his motives, wondering what else he had on his mind. Just my mention of Pauline's name had made his mouth twist in dislike. Yet, he could have been the person who was in Pauline's bedroom earlier in the afternoon before she died. That person didn't have to be a chef; that white jacket could have been left by either Robert or Nigel when they escorted Pauline home from the hospital. But why would Will have been there? He hadn't actually admitted that he got that letter from her. "I might have" was all he said. Did he want me back in his flat to get some more information from me? Was he worried about what I knew and was this sex approach just a ruse? I didn't want to find out today. I still felt threatened by him. He could change from charming to cold too quickly for my state of mind. Now, he was watching me too closely, not talking.

After I demolished a dish of mango ice cream to cool down my digestion, I thought I'd shake him a little by saying, "Speaking of poison, which Pauline seemed to feel you were handy with, you didn't by any chance send me any wonderful chocolate truffles, did you?" I'd still never gotten around to having those truffles analyzed. They were there in the freezer, tempting me.

He smiled a lazy, smug smile, but shook his head. I didn't believe him. Now I would have to find a lab and have the chocolates tested, just for my own peace of mind. Sending me chocolates with that note daring me to eat them was probably another evidence of his schoolboy humor. We finished our lunch with a definite chill between us, and I turned down his offer of a ride home in his car. I remembered that he also had a big black Jaguar. Was I being paranoid by thinking that maybe he wanted more than my body; maybe he really wanted to shut me up?

Chapter 20

The flat was clean, quiet and too empty when I got back from that strange lunch with Will. Because of my fight with Brack, it looked like I would be feeding myself this weekend instead of sharing great meals with him, so I had taken the underground the few stops to the flat, then stopped by my neighborhood Cullen's for necessary food. My mind had been so busy throughout the journey that when I noticed people eyeing me, I realized I was muttering, asking myself questions. Could I eliminate Will from my list of four men Pauline suspected of being at Fiona's flat that fatal evening, one of whom was her killer? Was he telling the truth about his alibi? Had he really cleared it with the police? That's what Brack had said, too. Were they both lying? I would have to call Inspector Reid on Monday and beg him to tell me all about Fiona's case and Will's alibi and Brack's, too. Maybe I could ask the American Embassy to put some pressure on the police here. I knew a friend of a friend there. As a detective, I was stymied and restless, waiting for the weekend to be over, and as a lonely woman I also wanted to get the weekend over and back to work.

As I put away the cheeses, bread and cokes in the fridge, I shook my head in amazement again at Will's actions. I've got to stop eating these cheeses—I'm hooked on Caerphilly—because I've put on at least two pounds. But the extra weight didn't seem to bother Brack, or Will, for that matter. I have to admit that, villain or no villain, Will was indeed a good-looking, sexy man, if you like that British, fair-haired, boyish look. I also had to admit that he had helped my self-esteem mightily after that fiasco with Brack. Lucille, you better admit, too, that he's probably trying to seduce you in order to find out more about the Sweet Whippo account—now his big rival. And don't forget that until you know for sure he was not involved in either death, you'd better not be too trusting. He could still be a killer.

But I now knew that Pauline had really sent out those four letters, with Will practically admitting to me that he had got one when he gave himself away by asking, "Who are the other three?" Brack was one, Will was the second, and now I had only two mystery men left. When I talked to Inspector Reid tomorrow, I would tell him that I would find out the other names. That would show him I was serious. And yes, I was going ahead with my Brack-despised detective work. I'd show him, I'd show everybody.

I walked into the sitting room and willed the telephone to ring. I had already checked and rechecked the Answerphone for messages. I picked up the telephone to call Brack, then put it back down. I wanted him to call me. Amazing what one lunch with a sexy man had done for my ego. I walked around the flat aimlessly and stood at the window looking at the leafy green trees of Hyde Park in the distance, wondering what was going to happen in my life now. Suppose Brack never came back. Well, Lucille, you did it yourself, so face the fact that the last few weeks of your stay in London may be Brackless. Then it's back to New York and Danny. Maybe not Danny. I couldn't quite see us going on in the old way. Too much had happened.

The telephone bell jolted me out of my reverie and it was

downright eerie to hear Danny's voice. He sounded different. Restrained. In the conversation that followed, we were polite with each other. Too polite. I began to realize that Danny had something to say to me, something he was having trouble getting out.

"Is something wrong?" I asked, fearful that disaster had struck family or friends.

"No, uh, I just wondered, Lucy, uh, are you almost finished with that job? I mean, will you be back soon or will you have to stay on?"

What was he getting at?

"Well, the work is about done here and nobody has said anything about extending the assignment." Danny didn't have to know how desperate I was to stay here. Near Brack.

"You like it over there, don't you?"

"Yes, I do; I really do." Could he have heard about Brack and me?

"Lucy, if you stay over there, what will happen to us?"

Long, long silence.

"I think something has happened to us, Danny." There, I'd said it.

I heard a sigh, a deep sigh, and then he said, "Maybe it's for the best. Things have changed here. I'm now sort of involved with someone else." Before I could respond, he hurried on. "You said we should live our own lives, but I didn't expect this to happen, and I wanted to talk to you first."

My first reaction was anger. Dumped by Danny? Good, old faithful Danny? But then I remembered that I was—or had been—involved with someone else. I steadied my voice and asked, "Anyone I know?"

"No, no. I met her at a party. Angela. She's from California, but you'd like her. I've told her all about you." He kept talking, saying he'd wanted to tell me face to face and so on, but I had stopped listening. A weariness took over. Danny wanted someone else, after all those years with me. Finally I said, "Danny, I think this is best. We'll talk again soon, but in the meantime, be happy." "You, too, Lucy," he said as I hung up. Now I really was alone. I walked to the window, gazing at the park, feeling sorry for myself, thinking about New York and Danny. Poor Lucille. But finally I had to admit that it was Brack and London that I really wanted. Stop this self pity, I told myself.

I moved away from the window and my eyes fell upon my computer, resting on the desk. It was time to do something constructive. At least I could sit down to do some work on my mystery novel. This poor book, the pages of which I had carefully packed and brought with me, had languished unread after my beginning burst of energy that came from just being in England again. I had promised myself I would finish it when I was in London. I had started it six months ago in New York City, after I had taken a writers' workshop. Yes, yet another writers' workshop. My plot—a couple of Americans traveling in England who get involved in a murder in a small, picturesque village— seemed such a good idea at the time, and I had convinced myself that my time in London would bring it to a conclusion, that I would sit happily at my computer practically every night, writing away. Instead, look what had happened. All the problems of working in London Office—and trying to stay alive and healthy—and my involvement with Brack had kept me from doing any real writing.

I sat down at the desk, pulled out the pages and started reading through it. God, it was awful, so stilted and artificial. What had possessed me to set a plot in a small English village, this little village I had spent just two weeks in three years ago, visiting a family friend? I would never be able to describe authentically that special ambiance of the village pub, the church, the cricket matches. Lucille, leave those villages to all the British mystery writers who do it so perfectly. And why was I writing about something I had dreamed up, when I was right in the middle of a real mystery? Remember that food poisoning on the very first day in London Office, those nasty notes that started coming on your second day there, Fiona's death, those chocolates you are convinced are poisoned and now Pauline's death! "Write about something you know," the workshop leader had preached. Well, I could certainly do that now. I picked up the pages of that manuscript, walked out to the kitchen and threw them into the rubbish bin. They were rubbish.

Then I sat down at the desk again, opened up the computer and started writing a whole new mystery, one that I could write from personal experience.

I would dedicate it to Pauline.

I made a list of all those things that had happened to me, put them in chronological order and put as much description around each event as I could remember. Then I made a list of the names of the people involved and since I certainly could not use their real names, it took me some time to make up new names and write them by the sides of the real ones. I wrote busily, the words coming easily as I set up a rough outline of the mystery. I was so pleased with myself. Then I stopped dead as I realized that I didn't know how this mystery would end or should end. Would my nosy detective work solve it? Or would I have to make up a totally different ending?

When the intercom buzzed, it took me a while to come back to reality.

"There's a delivery for you, Madam," the porter told me. "I'll send it up."

The knock on the front door came a moment later and a young man in slacks and sweater smiled as he handed me a shopping bag. "The man at the desk signed for it, Madam." He disappeared before I could figure whether to tip him.

It was a small but highly decorative carrier bag and when I reached into it, there it was. A box with glossy paper wrapping with a name scrolled across it. "Bentinck's," the name of the fancy confectioner's shop. I unwrapped it slowly, somehow knowing it would be a box of chocolates. Truffles. It was. And there was no card, no name. Will, I thought, Will did this. His idea of humor, teasing me, remembering that I had asked him if he'd sent me chocolates. I picked up one of the luscious cocoa-sprinkled chocolate balls, my mouth beginning to water, but then I stopped. I couldn't bite into it. I told myself it was not poisoned, it was fresh from Bentinck's, it was bound to be good. But I couldn't take that first savory bite. Suppose Will hadn't sent it? Suppose it wasn't fresh from Bentinck's, but from a used box with their name, a box filled with poisoned truffles? Was it just a coincidence that it arrived after that lunch? Suppose someone had seen Will and me at the restaurant and was counting on my thinking the box was from Will. Suppose . . . I put the truffle back, slammed the lid of the box down and walked quickly to the freezer, putting it way at the back. Next to the other box. I rang down to the porter and asked him if the messenger had been from Bentinck's. Joseph, our all-knowing porter, was silent for a moment, then said, "He wasn't in uniform, was he? Not like Bentinck's." Even as I looked up the shop's telephone number, I knew I wouldn't get any information from them. I was right. The polite but frosty voice told me they didn't give out the names of their clients. Clients! That did it for me. I couldn't take a chance. At least two of the four men on that list now knew that I had taken up Pauline's crusade and until I found out who the other two were, I was vulnerable.

I sighed and sat down at my computer, but I couldn't get back into the writing. I finally gave up. But I felt so good about getting some work done on the book that I rewarded myself with a gin and tonic, a salad, yet more cheese—after all, I had saved calories by not eating the chocolates—and a session with the television. I lay on the couch and watched a BBC mystery program carefully, trying to absorb the clever plotting. I went to my lonely bed, pleased with myself. I had almost forgotten about Brack. Almost.

The bad dreams came that night—in one I was standing at the edge of a whirlpool, in another I was being chased down a dark street by a shadowy figure, and in yet another I was looking in a shop window full of chocolates—and I awoke to the sound of heavy rain. We had been extremely lucky with the weather these past weeks, with sunshine almost every day—or at least part of every day—but now the traditional English wet weather had taken over. "Getting in practice for Wimbledon, of course," the BBC radio man said, but I decided it was really an omen for me to keep on working on my new mystery.

After breakfast I started in again, and this time the words came quickly as I related in fictional form the events that had happened since I first stepped off that jet at Heathrow. The good thing about fiction was that I could make anyone I want be the hero or the villain. My new plot had this good-looking, nice American woman—I made her a few years younger, of course—having to cope with such hostility from her own colleagues and getting involved in two deaths. No fiction there. While I worked away a strange thing happened. I couldn't keep the fiction separate from reality. The more I wrote, the more I stopped and thought about what was really happening. I could make my plot tidy, all the loose ends tied up, but in truth, nothing in real life was working out neatly at all. Still, I forced myself to keep writing for almost five hours, promising myself that the plot would unfold naturally. I stopped writing only to eat a sandwich, then got right back to work, I was so involved.

Then the telephone rang. It was Robert.

"Lucille, I'm so glad to find you at home. Do you think you could go with me to Pauline's flat where her sister is now? I promised her we would help her clean out some of the stuff Pauline left. She said she didn't want to throw away any company papers on her own and she didn't know anybody she could call on a Sunday, so I told her you could probably look at the recipes and things."

My spirits dropped when I heard Robert wanted me to go with him to see Pauline's grieving sister, but then inspiration came to me. I now had a legitimate reason to go through Pauline's desk and files to look for clues, clues that might tell me the names of the other men. What luck. I must have been silent so long, thinking this through, that Robert went on, anxiously.

"I know it's raining like hell, but Lucille, I need help with this. I don't know what should be saved or thrown away and I don't know how to get in touch with anyone from the test kitchen. I figured that with this rain, maybe your plans had changed."

They'd changed all right, but I was not going to tell Robert my sad tale.

"Don't worry, Robert, I'll be only too happy to help you.

I'm sure I could sort through Pauline's papers and pick out anything that the London office might want to have back."

There, didn't that sound generous of me? So we arranged to meet at Pauline's flat—again—right away.

I put on my raincoat and boots, added an umbrella and braved the rain. When I got to the flat, the front door was buzzed and I climbed up the stairs once again to Pauline's flat. I was greeted at the door by an older woman who resembled Pauline in her stocky build and fair hair. She relieved me of the coat, showed me where to put my boots and then led me inside.

"I'm Katherine Hopkins," she said, shaking me by the hand. "So kind of you to come. I'm in the midst of cleaning things out and I could do with some help. This bloody rain."

Robert came out from the kitchen, wiping his hands on a towel, and greeted me. I could see cartons on the countertop and dishes piled up on top of newspapers. I told Katherine how sorry I was about Pauline and she nodded her thanks.

"I can't believe my sister would do a thing like that," she said, her voice thick. "But then, we weren't that close. Pauline has lived in London for many years, and I saw too little of her, me having a big family and such. My husband is home with the children now, in Portsmouth, but I said I would come and identify her—" here she gave a small shudder "—and do something about the flat. The landlord is coming tomorrow, so in the meantime I've begun packing up things. Robert has been a wonderful help."

Robert looked down at the floor, his dark hair hanging over his eyes. I knew he was finding all this hard and I wondered again what had gone on between him and Pauline.

Katherine continued. "I don't know what to do with all

her papers, especially all that stuff from her office. She used to bring work home a lot. Every time I rang her in the evening, she seemed to be working away at her recipes. Could you sort these out and set aside what's important?"

I protested politely that I was not very knowledgeable about all of Pauline's work, just the material she had done for Sweet Whippo, but I was already moving toward the desk.

Katherine pointed toward a small stack of papers on top. "I've found the flat lease and some insurance papers and other things like that, but I haven't begun to look through all the drawers."

I had a flashback of that day, not too long ago, when Pauline and I went through Fiona's papers at her elegant flat after her death and I remembered too well how I had swiped the papers referring to S&C. Was I destined to be a thief again today? Could I justify stealing? Yes. I needed to know if Pauline had put any clues to that damning list of men somewhere in these papers. If I found any clue at all, I would gladly be a thief.

Katherine took Robert back into the kitchen and they started wrapping and packing things into those cartons. I could hear them talking about Pauline as I sat down at the desk, took a deep breath, opened the top drawer and pulled out a batch of papers.

Chapter 21

Pauline was fanatically neat with paper work, I soon discovered, as I started emptying the drawers in her desk and began looking at the papers. She also was a pack rat and had saved postcards, letters, theater playbills and countless other souvenirs, as well as every recipe she'd ever worked on for MWBV, it seemed to me. The recipes were obviously copies or drafts of ones in the files in the test kitchen and I shoved them aside. There were postcards and letters in one drawer that interested me most, and I started sorting through them quickly. I felt guilty, but not guilty enough to stop, although I didn't want Katherine to come back into the room and see me reading Pauline's personal mail. I came across a small bundle of cards and letters neatly kept together by a rubber band. When I flipped through them, my attention was caught. Apparently, Fiona, when off on trips, business or personal, would dash off a card or a one-page letter telling Pauline what was going on. Perhaps she didn't trust the telephone, fax or E-mail because of too many prying eyes. The dates were spread over the last few years, and although I searched closely for any familiar names (Brack's among them), the persons mentioned seemed to be in a sort of code. I mean, Fiona was clever enough to use nicknames for her companions on these trips, particularly when she was making disparaging remarks about them, which she obviously enjoyed doing. (I must remember to copy her idea because I have gotten in trouble in the past with memos and cards naming names that fell into the wrong hands.)

There were a series of postcards and letters from various cities in England—Fiona on a product introduction tour?—and pithy comments about somebody named "Monsieur Careme." One letter said, "Monsieur Careme just won't leave me alone. You know how these Francophiles are!" Another card said, "For once, French food comes second to me!" Lots of exclamation points. Dated two years back, covering about five days, the postcards usually showed scenes of the city they were currently in and the letters were on stationery from hotels involved. Thrifty, our Fiona. The cities visited were not exciting—Birmingham, Durham, Carlisle—but her personal life certainly was.

I puzzled on these for a while, then started looking for other cards and letters dated in sequence and I found four of these clipped together, all with comments about someone named "Gimpy." These were sent from Ireland three years ago and seemed to describe a vacation trip, not work. A one-page letter had several sentences, one saying, "His injuries don't slow him down too much in bed, thank God." Another said, "It's weird but challenging to be in bed with a man with both legs in plaster." I wondered what Pauline thought about these confidences. Was she living vicariously through Fiona's affair, and did the two women get together afterwards and laugh about the messages? I really wanted to take that little bunch of cards and letters back to the flat with me so I could read them carefully, but I had stupidly left my bag by the sofa, and before I could retrieve it I heard the voices of Robert and Katherine as they came toward the sitting room. I wrapped the rubber band around the cards and letters and shoved them into a drawer, shifting over quickly to the pile of recipes. I repeated the names of Monsieur Careme and Gimpy over and over in my mind to make sure I remembered them. I closed the drawers carefully and smiled at Pauline's sister.

"Unless you want to keep these for sentiment's sake, Katherine, I think I can safely say that there are copies in the files at our offices." There, that made it look like I'd been studying the recipes all this time.

"Well, I don't know what to do with them," Katherine admitted. "I tried some of the recipes she sent me once, but they are far too complicated for me and my family." She came over and looked down at the stack of papers, sighed, and then dropped them into the waste basket at the desk's side. Robert put down the heavy carton of Pauline's belongings by the door of the flat and wiped his hands on his pants.

"It's time for tea," Katherine announced and started off to the kitchen to prepare it.

A sudden thought made me call after her, "Were there any papers in the bedroom you want me to go through?" After all, Fiona had kept her damning documents in the bedside tables.

"No, dear," Katherine called back. "I've already looked there."

We drank our tea and ate a sandwich apiece made with an unidentified fishy filling from a little jar found in the cupboard. We talked about Pauline until we all became so depressed that I made excuses about work waiting and got Robert and me out of there. The poor guy had been much closer to Pauline than I had realized, and was so down that I asked him back to the flat for drinks and a thrown-together meal of pasta and salad. Sadly, I was on my own tonight, too. At the flat, he started pacing up and down, only stopping to stare out the big window at the rain coming down in sheets, until I remarked on it and asked him to please sit still somewhere. Robert's normally bright brown eyes were dull, his wavy dark hair hung lankly over his forehead and his spirits were so low that not even three gins and tonic cheered him up. At the table, I avoided the subject of Pauline and talked instead about the problems of thinking in metric terms for recipes and how different British food habits were.

"Do you think you'll ever get used to seeing beets in a tossed green salad?" I asked, trying to hit a light tone. "They call it beet root over here, slice it up and all it does is leak pink fluid over the lettuce."

"That's better than trying to learn to love Bubble and Squeak," he admitted. "Using day-old Brussels sprouts mixed with mashed potatoes is not my idea of utilizing leftovers. Oh, and I tried making Spotted Dick with Sweet Whippo the other day. Ugh."

"Spotted Dick? There's a recipe actually called Spotted Dick? Sounds unspeakably vulgar," I said with a shudder.

"Tastes unspeakably vulgar," he admitted. "Sweet Whippo was hopeless there. It seemed to dissolve the raisins into a dark, gooey mess."

Talk like this got us through dinner and up to coffee. Now was the time to pump Robert.

"Did Pauline ever mention the names 'Careme' or 'Gimpy' in any of her conversations over the past weeks?" I asked casually as I came out of the kitchen.

"Careme and who?" he asked, accepting a mug of black coffee.

"Gimpy. I think they were nicknames for friends of Fiona. She liked to give her pals and perhaps lovers these

207

nicknames." I wondered if either of those names fitted Brack. No, she probably had her own special name for him. And would he ever call me again? I had checked the Answerphone when Robert was in the kitchen getting ice, out of earshot. Still no messages.

Robert pondered my words for a while and then shook his head. "I never heard Pauline mention those names. But, historically, Careme was a famous French chef, one of the first professionals."

"Of course. I should have remembered that name from my cooking classes. I thought it sounded familiar. A French chef, eh?"

"Celebrated. And doesn't 'Gimpy' mean crippled? Seems to me I've heard that word used for people who limp."

I got up and went over to the bookcase, took out a dictionary and sure enough, it said a "gimp" (origin unknown) was a cripple, one who limped.

"Why are you so interested in those nicknames, Lucy?" Robert asked me, looking over the top of his mug.

"I don't know exactly, Robert. It's one of my crazy ideas."

"Pauline told me you were helping her find Fiona's murderer. Are you going to keep on doing that? I think you should, for Pauline, I mean. It meant everything to her."

I was surprised and wondered how many people Pauline had told that I was helping her. If so, it left me in an awkward position. If Robert expected me to go on, did other people think that way? Could I really come through on this case? No matter what happened, it was all grist for my mystery novel. Does that sound callous?

I quizzed him. "Did she tell you whom she suspected? I mean, she must have talked to you about her suspects."

"No, she didn't. She said I wasn't even over here when Fiona was killed, and so she didn't want to involve me. She acted kind of funny about the whole situation, was very mysterious about it. Nigel told me he thought she was obsessed with Fiona and her death, and was acting crazy. Crazier than usual, he said, not very nice of him. He said some people thought the two were lovers."

Not bloody likely, I thought, not from what I had heard and read about Fiona and her men. But what did I know? I also didn't want to tell the poor man that Nigel had a point about Pauline's mental state. Even Brack thought she'd gone round the bend over Fiona's death. I also didn't want to mention Will Hammersmith's comment that Nigel had been on their S&C team. I would look into that tomorrow, even though Will was probably just lying, trying to cause friction and mess up my campaign.

Robert said he was feeling better as he gathered up his raincoat and umbrella, promising to work even harder on the remaining weeks of the Sweet Whippo campaign to get his mind off Pauline.

"Oh by the way, Robert, did you send me a box of truffles yesterday?" I had to make sure.

"Truffles?" He was obviously puzzled. "No. Was it for the next press intro? Should I have?"

"Nope. It's just that I got some yesterday with no card."

"Braxton Clark, probably," he said firmly. "Everyone knows about you two."

I didn't want to go into my problems with Brack, so I just nodded and closed the door.

First thing the next morning I rang Inspector Reid. He was out of town and I had to be content to leave an urgent message. I spent the morning in meetings, so had no time to call Nigel or ask around about those nicknames, but when Jane and I went out to the Red Lion for lunch, I started questioning her. The noise level was so high I practically had to shout.

"Did you ever hear Fiona call one of her friends or colleagues Gimpy?"

Jane put down her cheese and chutney sandwich and looked at me, puzzled.

"Sorry? It's so noisy in here. Did you say 'Grumpy'?"

"No, no, I said 'Gimpy.' I can't tell you why this is important, but somebody told me that Fiona always had little nicknames for people, for people she worked with, maybe."

Jane took a sip of her wine and started taking bites of her sandwich, her face contorted in thought. Then she swallowed and said, "That sounds like Fiona all right. Imagine calling someone Gimpy."

"I don't think she did it to his face," I said. "Just when she was talking to Pauline. (I substituted "talking" for the word "writing," because then I would have to explain how I knew about Fiona's correspondence.)

Jane smiled and shook her head. "You're not still working on Pauline's theory of Fiona's being killed, are you? Our Miss Marple of MWVB."

Did everyone in the office know that I was now seriously playing detective? Did that put me at risk?

"Well, you know how I feel about mysteries, and I told you I was trying to write one myself. Pauline did leave me with some intriguing ideas and I need to learn more."

Jane shook her head sadly and took another bite, lost in thought. A silence fell, then she finished off her glass of wine, put the glass down on the table with a thud and said, "You know, you've started me thinking. All I can say is that Gimpy might well be a man who Fiona was supposed to be involved with. There was this chap, one of the panelists with her on a telly cookery show, that had this car crash and barely survived. He had to use crutches for ever so long. It was all in the papers a few years ago and then he finally showed up on the box walking with his Zimmer frame." She saw my puzzled look and explained, "You call them 'walkers.' He's the only man that might fit that description. Was considered quite a hero."

"What happened to him?"

"Let me think. I seem to remember hearing that he went to Australia. Warm climate and all that for his health."

"Was he a chef?"

"No, I don't think so, but I think he was high up in some hotel and restaurant chain. Supposed to be one of these gourmet experts on wine and food. I remember that Fiona was always dropping his name in meetings. I sincerely hope she didn't call him Gimpy to his face. He was dishy, I remember. There, Miss Marple, I've given you a clue." She looked around at the crowd, busy eating, drinking and talking at the tops of their lungs, then back at me and added, "In the meantime, we've got work to do, if you can spare the time from your private eye work."

I could tell I wasn't being taken very seriously by Jane. But if this were the same man, I figured I could eliminate him from Pauline's list of suspects. No I couldn't, because he could easily have been back to England on that fateful Sunday. I would have to get his real name and see if anybody at the office was still in touch with him.

"Jane, could you try to remember his name and then find out if anyone has seen him lately? It's important to me."

She gave me a fishy eye, but shrugged and said she would ask around. "You're very serious about this, I see, but I hope you know what you are doing. You're liable to

211

step on some people's toes and make yourself very unpopular," she warned as we gathered our bags and left the pub.

At this point in my life, more unpopularity really didn't matter, so I went right ahead.

Now for "Careme," "Monsieur Careme." I decided I wouldn't ask Jane about this, because she'd probably start in on me for being obsessed with weird names, but instead I would take myself down to the test kitchens and talk to the women there. They had culinary training and would probably recognize the name. We had all been working closely on Sweet Whippo together and Pauline's staff had turned out to be friendly and not the troublemakers I thought they would be when I had first met them. Perhaps they felt guilty for my getting so sick at that first Sweet Whippo taste testing, but Fiona had never told me which woman had been the one who left those delicacies out of the fridge all night.

When I knocked and opened the door to their kitchens, Nirma, a young Indian woman, was on her own, sitting at the center table, eating yoghurt from a bowl and reading a magazine. She looked up, obviously surprised to see me dropping in like this, and started to get up.

"Please," I said, "go on with your lunch. I'm sorry to interrupt. I just wanted to talk a little, you know, about Pauline."

She politely closed the magazine, put the yoghurt aside and folded her hands, resting them on the table. Her face, which was usually wreathed in a smile, with her white teeth shining against her dark skin, was solemn. She was wearing a white apron over her dark orange silk sari.

"I miss her, we all miss her very much. She was good to us, taking over after Miss Gordon died," she said, looking down at her folded hands. "Is it true, she was a suicide?"

"That's what the police think. I prefer to think that she mixed too many pills and accidentally overdosed herself."

"She was very upset these last few days," Nirma said. "Very distracted, in fact, very edgy and used to jump when the telephone rang. We tried to get her to calm down, take time off, but she seemed driven. Yes, driven."

I nodded sadly and then went on.

"I saw her sister Katherine yesterday and helped her go through some papers from the office here. She had kept lots of recipes that she'd been working on."

Nirma nodded. "She took work home almost every night. Even before Miss Gordon's death."

"She had some recipes and papers that had the names 'Careme' and 'Gimpy' on them. Do you know who these people are? Were they clients?" I asked, offhand.

Nirma looked blank and then screwed up her face in apparent thought. " 'Careme' we studied about at cookery school. He was one of the first professional French chefs, very well known, in fact, he cooked for the Prince Regent here in Brighton for a time. But I know of no client by that name. I could look in the files for you." She jumped up, gracefully moving her skirt aside to walk to a chest-high file drawer, where she started flipping through the files. "Here's the list of current clients," she said, handing it to me. I looked at it, but there was no Careme. Nirma was still searching the files and then handed me another list. "Here is a list of clients for the last five years. I have only been here for a few months, so I didn't work on these accounts."

The door opened then and Caro, the Japanese woman on Pauline's staff, walked in. She stopped, surprised, then nodded to Nirma and came in. She was a petite woman, a few years older than Nirma, competent and self possessed.

"Hello, Miss Anderson. Do you need something from

us? Can we help you?" she asked, her round face anxious as she opened a cabinet and put her handbag and a plastic carrier bag in it. She wore a plain dark skirt and a light pink blouse. No exotic native dress for her.

"No, Caro, not really. I came down to talk about Pauline, to say how sorry we all are."

She nodded. "Everything is chaotic, is it not? No Ms. Gordon, no Mr. Hammersmith and now no Pauline. We will try to handle things, though." She looked around the room and saw the open file cabinet. She started toward it.

Nirma spoke up quickly. "Miss Anderson was also asking about clients."

"Clients?"

I didn't want to go through the story all over again, but merely said, "I'm interested in a client from a few years ago named Careme. Not the famous French chef, but someone that Fiona Gordon called that. Sort of a nickname."

She gave an odd little tinkly laugh. "Careme? A client? Oh no, not a client." She looked at me, her bright black eyes shining. She smiled, evidently enjoying a joke of her own. "Oh no indeed, not a client." She stood there, still smiling. Then she took the list from my hand and looked down at it, then handed it back to Nirma. She looked up at me, obviously still amused.

" 'Monsieur Careme' was indeed a nickname for one of Miss Gordon's friends, who worked with her on several accounts a couple of years ago, a British chef who was so fond of French cookery that we teased him about it. Everything had to be French, always French, then. Yet he was English, very English, but he had trained and worked in restaurants in Paris. Ah yes, we ribbed him about it all the time and Miss Gordon called him 'Monsieur Careme' in front of us, when we working on recipes for a big nationwide tour. Always those French dishes. They spoke French together."

She turned and went over to a refrigerator, opened it, took out a big bowl and put it on the table. She smiled at me again. "Please excuse me, but I must get on with this recipe. Not Sweet Whippo, though." She reached for an apron hanging on a peg nearby.

I was standing very still, hardly breathing, waiting to hear who this chef was, the man who could well be the man that Pauline had sent her accusing letter to, but Caro was taking her own sweet time telling me.

She looked at me, shook her head slightly and said, "We did laugh at him behind his back most of the time, because Miss Gordon was so amusing. Once I saw him get so angry at her for teasing him that he threw a big spoon at her and hit her on the shoulder. That's when she realized that she should not make fun of him any more and even stopped talking French to him." She picked up the bowl, took the plastic wrap off it and sniffed it. She looked into it carefully and then sniffed it again. Then she put it down on the table and turned to me.

"You know him, too, but not as Monsieur Careme. Oh, no, you know him as Chef Nigel Newton!"

My face must have shown my shock because Cara giggled and said, "Have I surprised you? Of course it was just a little joke of Ms. Gordon's, but since her death, Pauline didn't use that name. I think she thought it bad taste, now. Besides, she was fond of him, too."

I couldn't seem to think straight. I never somehow expected Nigel to be one of Fiona's lovers, but then again, why not? According to those cards and letters from Fiona to Pauline that I read through, they must have been on a product introduction trip together a couple of years ago and had been sleeping together then and perhaps later. "Mon-

215

sieur Careme" would certainly hear from me and soon to answer my question about a letter from Pauline. He also needed to explain what connection he had to S&C. Something here in this tangle of people was eluding me.

I smiled and nodded, pretending that I was amused at my ignorance about Nigel, and we talked a little more about Pauline before I took my departure. I thanked both Cara and Nirma and started for the door. When I turned to look back and smile, I saw them both standing there, watching me. I knew they were just waiting for me to close the door behind me before the talking began about this strange American woman so interested in Fiona Gordon's men friends.

When I got back to my desk, I had to put aside any thoughts of following up on Nigel and on "Gimpy" while I sat through yet another meeting about our next Sweet Whippo launch in Bristol. I still hadn't heard from Brack and so I swallowed my pride—again—and called him at his office later, only to hear his secretary Joan say he was away from the office for a few days. Where was he? She wouldn't say. I was dumped, obviously. Now all those empty evenings stretched ahead. All I could do was spend them on my mystery.

Jane stuck her head around the door later in the afternoon with a smug smile on her round, freckled face.

"Just thought I'd let you know that I tracked down poor old Gimpy. Man named Rogerson. Seems he did move to Australia, married a woman there and is now running a fancy hotel in Melbourne. In fact, I just spoke to him there. He hasn't been back to England for two years. He swore that to me."

I was astonished. "How did you know where to find

him? And did you really talk to him?"

"I have my sources, you know. Two can play at this mystery game." She shook her red curls in mock despair and grinned at me. She wouldn't tell me how she found all this out except to add, "I have agents in Australia, you know. Incidentally I charged the call to the Sweet Whippo account, okay?"

She was still treating the whole thing as a joke, a joke on me and my amateur sleuthing. But at least I could forget about Gimpy. The names on Pauline's list of possible killers were now Will Hammersmith, Nigel Newton and yes, Braxton Clark.

I rang Inspector Reid again because I had to check the alibis of Will and Brack, but again had no luck. I insisted on talking to his deputy and told the poor man my story all over again. He was polite, but even the urgency in my voice didn't move him. He did agree, however, to pass my questions on to his boss as soon as it was possible. So that left me wondering about Nigel. Had he been interviewed by the police and his alibi checked?

The more I sat and thought, the more I realized that although I had been working with Nigel for several weeks, I really didn't know anything about him. Now I had learned that Nigel was a former lover of Fiona, according to those letters from her to Pauline. He was Monsieur Careme. Will had said that Nigel had been hired to work on S&C, working closely with Fiona, perhaps. Was he the man that she had been expecting that fatal night? Nigel had also wanted to visit Pauline in the hospital; he could have been the mystery visitor before I showed up. Then he had gone along with Robert to fetch her from the hospital and take her back to her flat. Nigel was a chef. It could have been his white jacket on that kitchen stool in Pauline's flat. He could have gone back to her flat and was hiding in the bedroom. Caro had said Pauline was fond of him, but she sounded frightened when I was there.

How could I find out the connection between Fiona and Nigel? How could I find out his relationship with Pauline? All I knew was that I was suddenly excited about this turn of events and I knew I had to, just had to, talk to Nigel. But I must not let him know that I now knew all these things. Instead, I would say that it was important to talk about Sweet Whippo. I called Nigel at his house, told him that I had some problems to work out with him on our Bristol launch and I would like to come over right now. He was reluctant at first, talking about having to do some extra work for another account this afternoon, but I insisted. He finally gave in and I locked away all my papers in the bottom drawer and set out.

Chapter 22

Nigel greeted me politely at the door and led me through the house and into his vast kitchen, saying he had told me he was in the midst of some necessary recipe development and would I mind terribly if he went on with it? I saw no sign of his assistant Paul and when I asked, he said he'd sent him to Fortnum's for boar pâté. Nigel was in his work clothes: a maroon sweatshirt, dark jeans covered by a clean blue-and-white striped chef's apron and a stained dish towel tucked into the apron strings in front. No chef's toque, but his dark straight hair was still neatly held in a little pigtail. He had designer stubble on his usually clean-shaven face, which made him look different, almost raunchy, not like the reserved, competent British chef I'd worked with these past weeks.

My plan was to discuss Sweet Whippo plans and to cleverly inject some talk of Fiona and Pauline so I could find out if Nigel was that fourth man on Pauline's list. I could then take my list of suspects—even with Brack's name on it—to Inspector Reid to show him I'd followed up on Pauline's suspicions as I wanted to do—whether or not he approved—and convince him to check the statements again of each person. Then my part would be finished. Pauline would be vindicated if one man's alibi wouldn't hold up. I had to believe that Brack was innocent. Had to.

Nigel gestured toward a high stool by the side of his butcher block-topped work table and I climbed on it, only to discover that I was gazing at a pig's head lying there staring at me with open eyes.

"Need to make some brawn right away for a super dish," he said, when he saw my look of horror. I turned away when he applied his knife to scoop out the pig's eyes. But not before I saw him put the objects into a dish and then into the nearby refrigerator. "The Asians love those eyes," he said, shaking his head in wonder.

"Now to cook piggy for a few hours," he said, adding the head to a steaming cauldron of water on his big stove, "and turn those brains to jelly. There you are, piggy," he said, wiping his hands on the towel. I didn't want to ask him what brawn was, but I found out anyhow when he said, "You Yanks call it head cheese," and cleaned off the board carefully, wiping it with yet another stained towel. Didn't chefs ever use clean towels?

He looked up at me, smiled at my obvious discomfort and asked, "What's so important that it warrants a visit from you? Not bad news about Sweet Whippo, I hope? I thought the campaign was going brilliantly. We got plenty of coverage of our media intro, didn't we? Here, where are my manners? Let me get you a drink. I just made some Pimm's Cup Punch for another client, and a glass or two won't be missed while you give me your taste test opinion."

He took a pitcher from the refrigerator, reached behind him in a cupboard for a bottle of gin and poured a sizeable amount in the pitcher, stirred it with a long handled spoon and filled a glass. It was a pink mixture with raspberries and some other unidentifiable fruit floating around.

"See what you think of that," he said, handing me the glass.

I took a sip, made a little face because of its bitterness, but drank more. It just might give me courage to ask the right questions. The gin would certainly help.

"Too bitter for my American taste, but refreshing," I reported. "I do need to kick a few ideas around, ideas for the Bristol launch, which we face next week."

"I'm all ears, but you'll have to forgive me if I'm not at my best. I simply must get this recipe development done. It's for a new restaurant where I'm acting as consultant."

Nigel smiled smugly, reached under the worktable and brought out a large red onion. Still looking straight into my eyes, he started doing that rapid chopping of the onion without looking at it—the act that every chef on television does to impress his viewers. Culinary Television 101, I call it, and I secretly hope some day a chef will miss and chop a finger off in full view of his admiring audience, but somehow, I didn't think that Nigel would indulge me today. I leaned back a little so that the onion wouldn't make me weep. It didn't seem to bother him as he went on chopping, humming under his breath. The red onion slices piled up, like little pools of blood. Why was I thinking of blood? I started again, keeping a businesslike tone to my voice.

"I heard that S&C is coming out sooner than planned with their new product. Have you heard anything?"

He stopped, both hands still, fixing me with his shiny brown eyes.

"How did you hear that? Oh, yes, I heard you and Hammersmith were seen, heads together over chapatis at a local Paki palace, just last Saturday. Sleeping with the enemy, are we?"

News obviously traveled fast in the London Foodie Mafia.

"Not yet," I responded, unruffled. "But he did tell me

more than I wanted to hear about some people and their involvement with S&C. Like you."

He didn't blink an eye and simply shrugged. "Hammersmith talks too much, but if you're worried about me and my former time with S&C, never fear. My whole being is now devoted to Sweet Whippo. I don't know one single thing about S&C's new plans because I have no connection with him or his company anymore. Believe me."

"I want to."

I had to, actually. While I was working on my next question, Nigel went to the walk-in freezer at the end of the kitchen, disappeared into it and reappeared with the frozen carcass of some animal which he slapped down on a back counter. "Thaw away, little lamb," he said. I had this sudden mental image of Nigel talking personally to various ingredients all day long. He picked up another big knife and added some shiny purple eggplants to his block and began slicing them neatly.

"What were you saying, Lucille?"

"Robert and I are rethinking the Bristol launch. Could you substitute something a little less French and more basic British for one your recipes? I'm told the women there resist London gourmet ideas." It sounded weak and we both knew it.

"Where did you hear that?" He shook his head. "You were obviously misled. After all, the women in Bristol watch television and see all the cookery programs. I'm sure they've seen plenty of gourmet cooking. I did a series a couple of years ago on French cooking and some of our best response was from the southwest. Actually, I was quite a celebrity then."

"Known as Monsieur Careme?" I asked. He'd given me an unexpected opening.

He stood stock still, knife poised over the eggplant. "Where did you hear that?"

"From Pauline. Apparently, that was Fiona's nickname for you."

"Fiona did love those little nicknames for her lovers. I wonder what she called your Braxton."

That hurt, but I let it pass.

"Yes, we did have our little fling," he admitted. "Fiona liked to brag, I'm afraid, and Pauline was a willing listener. Not a healthy relationship. Both of them in their own little world."

"And now both dead."

"Pity," he said coldly. "But I'm not surprised that Pauline topped herself. Been heading that way for a long time, popping pills for donkeys' years and Fiona always covering for her, you know." He swept the onion and eggplant into a pan, put it aside, picked up another eggplant and started cutting it, not looking at me.

"About Bristol and those Froggy recipes. Shall I talk to Robert and see what he thinks?" he asked. "Or perhaps we could ring him now." He was baiting me.

"No, let's go over a few points here. Then we'll see what Robert thinks." I refused to be bluffed.

"Right. As you can see, I am busy, but let's get on with Sweet Whippo."

"I thought we might substitute something else for the Rice Crèmes," I said.

"You mean the ones that Pauline said made her sick? Bollocks. Nothing wrong with them, it was because she was popping all those pills and drinking champers."

"I know, I know. But I also checked the dessert carts—sorry, sweets trolley—afterwards and they were the only things left, so why don't we think of something new? Gingerbread maybe?"

"Too boring." He closed his eyes and thought for a moment, then opened them and nodded. "But I will consider candied ginger used in a pudding. Yes, that might do it. Too bad Pauline won't be here to taste it. She loved her puds."

"Poor Pauline. Everyone thinks I am being too nosy about Fiona and Pauline's deaths." I could see his head nodding, but I went on. "I do feel an obligation to Pauline to carry on her crusade to find justice for Fiona because it meant so much to her. She made me promise to keep up her investigations."

He straightened up and stood there, knife in hand, skepticism written all over his face.

"I can see you don't believe me," I said calmly, "but she confided a great deal in me, you know. Told me all kinds of new things, even on the day she died, the day she came home from the hospital. I was at her flat that afternoon, you know." I looked closely at him to see if this statement would rattle him. Was he the visitor hidden in her bedroom? He didn't change expression, just kept busy lining up his eggplants and onions in neat rows. "She even had a list of suspects for Fiona's death she wanted me to interview," I said boldly. "She had sent a letter to each of them and a letter and copy of the list to the police, too."

He stopped cutting then, looked up at me sharply, frowned, then gave a forced laugh, looking down at his butcher block again, scooping up the pieces of vegetables and dropping them in a pan. "I wouldn't give much thought to Pauline and her list," he said. "She was known to be bonkers and you're certainly not going to make any friends by going around chatting up suspects. And as for our fearless Metropolitan police, most of them can't even read.

Here, I forgot to top up your drink." He looked at the half-filled glass I was holding and shook his head. "You're acting like it's poison." He turned away, opened the refrigerator, took out the pitcher and put it on the table right in front of me, folded his arms across his chest and stood watching me.

Poison. Why did he say "poison?" I sensed a sudden change in the atmosphere, a difference in Nigel. Here I thought I was being a smart Jessica Fletcher with my questions but I was beginning to feel threatened. I had only wanted to find out if Nigel had got one of those letters and then present the evidence to Inspector Reid, but somehow Nigel seemed to be challenging me. Was I being smart or stupid? Forget about poison, Lucille. It's just your vivid imagination taking over. Stick to a few more Sweet Whippo questions and get the hell out of here. Then I looked at that sharp knife he had picked up again running his thumb lovingly over its sharp edge and I thought, one quick thrust from him and I could be sliced up and bleed to death under his cold eyes. Calm down, Lucille.

"Drink up," Nigel said, as he filled my glass, then stood there watching me with a little smile. A smug little smile.

I took the glass up to my lips, took a tiny sip, then put it back down. I was definitely getting edgy and very suspicious. "Not my kind of drink," I said firmly.

Nigel merely shrugged and looked up over my head at the big rack of copper pots and pans hanging there, muttering about needing just the right pan for this recipe. Involuntarily, I twisted and looked up following his eyes and there was a huge copper pan, its shiny sides reflecting the kitchen's bright lighting, hanging on the steel rack, right overhead, just waiting for me. If that cracked down on my head, helped along by Nigel, he would surely tell the police it was just a tragic accident. What's wrong with you, Lucille? You're turning this kitchen into a dungeon. I slid carefully off the stool and stood up to get out of his way as he came around the table and reached up for a long-handled heavy pot. He banged it down on the tabletop, making me jump. He smiled at my action, saying, "Jumpy, aren't we?" Then he walked toward the freezer. "Excuse me, I must nip in here," he said, as he disappeared into its maw.

My mind suddenly pictured *me* in that freezer, locked in and slowly dying a cold, cold death. I reached down slowly and carefully to the floor, picked up my bag by its long straps and started to edge by the stove toward the door to the kitchen. I just wanted out. Now.

Nigel reappeared, holding a sheet of some kind of pastry, stopped by the big pot of boiling water holding that pig head, stirred it with a big wooden spoon, looked up at me and said, "Boiling hot, just right."

Boiling hot water, I thought, taking a step back away from the stove. If that pot turned over on me, I was a goner. I started backing toward the door, trying to figure out how to make a dignified exit when all I really wanted to do was turn and run. Suddenly I didn't want to be a clever detective any more.

He put the sheet of flaky pastry on the counter in back, picked up a towel and started wiping off the chopping block. "Don't go, Lucille. Sorry that I haven't been able to give you my full attention. Now let's see, what were you saying about Fiona? Oh, yes, Fiona had her admirers, you know, including me—for a time. Monsieur Careme. We were both into our French period then. She didn't like to let go of any man, liked to keep them under her thumb, and she did fancy herself, you know, wearing those spike heels. No wonder she couldn't keep her balance. Silly woman, all dressed up in fancy black pajama pants, with that ridiculous frilly white blouse, thought she was nineteen years old." He stopped suddenly and looked at me, a strange expression on his face.

I was stunned. He'd said, "Couldn't keep her balance." Was he talking about that fatal night? Oh yes, he was there, or how else could he know what Fiona had been wearing? I could not recall anyone mentioning that blouse, not Pauline, not Inspector Reid, not Will. Brack had told me that the police had told him that Fiona was wearing wide, flared pants, but he had said nothing about a frilly white blouse.

There was this silence now, neither one of us saying anything. I was afraid to meet his eyes, afraid he would read in them my question. I quickly moved toward the door, holding my bag close to my side.

"Nigel, I won't take up any more of your time. Just let me know about the new recipes and I'll talk to Robert. Thanks for the Pimm's, and I'll be off." I said all this in a rush of words, but he quickly came from behind the worktable and got between me and the door. He took off the towel from his waistband, stretched it out and twirled it, and for a minute I thought he was going to strangle me with it, but after a moment, he merely tossed it on a chair.

"Lucille, I do apologize for my inattention, but I am very, very busy. Now let me walk you to the door and get you a taxi. I know you want to get on with Sweet Whippo. And your investigations." This last was said in a sneering voice as he put his hand on my arm. I kept myself from recoiling and let him propel me out of that deadly kitchen.

"No, no, I don't need a taxi, I want to walk, I have some errands on the Kings Road, don't bother," I babbled, not meeting his eyes.

In silence we walked through the house toward the front

door. His hand tightened on my arm so much that it hurt.

When we got to that blessed front door, he finally let go of me as he pulled open the heavy door. I walked out, stumbled on the doorstep, righted myself and shook off his helping hand. I mumbled my goodbyes quickly and went down the front walk to the street. I didn't look back until I was on the sidewalk when I turned to wave goodbye politely. He was still standing on the doorstep, watching me. He didn't wave back.

Chapter 23

I walked rapidly, knees wobbling slightly, down the street to the Kings Road, trying to regain my composure. I forced myself not to look back, fearful that Nigel might be coming after me, ready to grab me and force me back into that lethal kitchen. As soon as I got to the Kings Road, I hailed a taxi and gave the driver the address of the police station where Inspector Reid worked. I had his card clutched in my sweaty hand, rescued from my handbag's clutter. No more telephone calls. This had to be face to face.

The man behind the reception desk at the station was patient and polite, told me Detective Inspector Reid was in his office, but was busy and couldn't see me and I should go away and telephone to make an appointment.

I lost my cool. "No way," I said. "I must see him right away." When that didn't work, I added, "This is about murder, not about a lost dog." My voice was loud and the sight and sound of this noisy woman prompted action, because suddenly Inspector Reid appeared.

He was very proper, saying, "Will you come through, please," but hustled me back to his small office, while I babbled away. On the way there, he stopped briefly, turned to a policemen who was openly fascinated by this scene to say, "Tea, in my office, right away." Tea—the Brit's answer to any crisis, including a demanding American woman.

Actually, I had calmed down by the time we got to his office and had put my thoughts in order. He seated me in a chair, walked around to sit down behind his desk, said he was sorry he hadn't had a chance to get back to me, but he had been unusually busy, then asked me to begin.

I explained everything very succinctly, I thought, and when I got to the part about the white frilly blouse, Inspector Reid shuffled through the files on his desk, pulled out a thick one, and sorted through the papers until he found a photograph which he pored over. I reached for it, but he wouldn't show it to me. I pulled my hand back, chastised.

"Hmmm," he said. Just "hmmm." A young man in uniform came in with the tea, and I took the cup handed me, and took a sip. It was awful. I don't like milk and sugar in my tea. My hand was steady as I held the cup, though, and I was proud of that.

I talked on and he made copious notes. Finally, unusual for me, I ran out of talk. He rose, came around the desk and helped me up, signaling that this meeting was over.

"Now what do I do?" I asked. I was truly angry that he was treating this startling revelation of mine so calmly. "I realize that you may have more important things to investigate, but I think this *was* murder. Should I go with you to Nigel's and we can face him together? Make him tell you what he told me?" See how brave I was now, now that I could have a police escort?

Inspector Reid flinched. "No, no, please, do nothing, I beg you. We will follow up on this immediately. Just go back to your flat and we will be in touch with you."

He escorted me through the station as fast as was decent, ignoring the curious looks of the staff, and got me a taxi. I was even angrier now. Not even an admiring word from him about my clever way of getting the truth from Nigel. I got in the taxi, slammed the door, looked straight ahead and gave the driver the flat's address. Reid said something to me through the open window, but I ignored it, refusing to look at him.

Home at last, I locked the front door behind me, put on the chain and then went into kitchen and made sure the door to the service hall was locked. I didn't really think Nigel would come around to continue our conversation. He was probably still boiling that pig's head, thinking poor old Lucille was just getting as paranoid as Pauline. But I took no chances.

"Where is that smart fearless detective of yesteryear, Lucille?" I asked aloud as I found myself pacing up and down on the expensive oriental rug in the sitting room, staring down at its patterns and colors. "Get a grip. Do something normal, like eating dinner."

Whenever I get really upset, I find it soothing to cook and eat my favorite comfort foods, but when I looked in the fridge, I found nothing but more cheese, some moldy bacon and a six bottles of Mexican beer. Ah, but that beer reminded me that in the freezer there was a big container of chili I had cooked and carefully stored a week ago, chili I was going to dazzle Brack with, served with the icy beer. I had promised to show him real chili, not this weak, bean-clogged British stuff. But wait, it would be perfect to soothe my jumpy nerves tonight, maybe just one bowl of it, and save the rest. See, I was still hopeful about Brack.

Back in New York City, I was noted for my celebrated chili, made by a recipe from a Texas friend and done from scratch—finely chopped chunks of beef (not ground meat), minced onions, hot, hot, hot chili powder, cumin, canned Italian tomatoes, salt, garlic and finally cornstarch for thickening. No beans. Beans were considered stretchers and frowned upon by my purist Texas friend. I had even added a little of the really hot chili powder from the Indian grocery on the corner to this batch. Now, they knew hot!

I zapped the container briefly in the microwave to thaw the chili soft enough to turn out into a pot, added more water and put it on the stove, turning the gas up high. I prefer old-fashioned slow cooking for chili, rather than re-heating it completely in the micro. Soon it was bubbling away merrily as I stirred it carefully with a big wooden spoon. The pot was a heavy copper one with a long handle and just looking at it reminded me of that monster pot that had hung on the rack over my head in Nigel's kitchen. Forget it, Lucille. That's all over. Trust the Metropolitan Police to go to Nigel's house, interview him and find out if and what he did to Fiona. You did your part for Pauline and you showed the Met police your clever American detective ways.

While the chili was cooking, I telephoned Brack at home and got that damn answering machine. But this time I left a message, spoken through slightly clenched teeth.

"You might be interested to know that Chef Nigel is in deep shit. It's too complicated to explain, but it seems *he* was the man who was at Fiona's flat that night she went down those stairs. I've told the police and they are heading there to talk to him. Right away, I hope. So now you don't have to listen to any more nosy questions from me. Lucky you. Goodbye."

I know it was childish but I felt much better afterwards.

I went back to the kitchen and my chili. I kept stirring, trying not to think of Brack. The wonderful spicy, smoky aroma filled the air of the small kitchen and it suddenly made me homesick, thinking of how many times I had made this dish in my New York apartment. Well, I would be back there before too long, mission accomplished here.

The telephone on the kitchen wall rang, startling me. I started toward it.

"Damn," I said, as my elbow hit the wooden spoon and knocked it to the floor. Of course the spoon had to be full of chili and make a big mess on the kitchen floor. I stepped gingerly around it and got to the phone. It was Robert.

"Lucille, I've just seen Katherine off at Waterloo. She had to go back home even though she hasn't finished clearing out Pauline's flat. I tried to get hold of you earlier but you'd left the office."

I had completely forgotten about Pauline's sister Katherine and my half-hearted promise to Robert to go out to dinner with them. In fact, I had completely forgotten that I should have called and told Robert about Nigel the minute I got home since he was so eager for me to carry on Pauline's crusade. I'd been too obsessed with Brack.

"Sorry, Robert, but I had to go to Nigel's house. You're not going to believe what happened there but I need to talk to you. It's serious, deadly serious. Maybe you should come over. Please. I've even got some Texas chili for you."

" 'Serious, deadly serious.' What are you talking about, Lucille? You're not making sense!"

"I'll tell you all about it when you get here. Please. Right away."

He said he had to stop by his hotel, but would show up as soon as he could. I heaved a sigh of relief and felt better. I needed someone here badly, and it would be nice to have a fellow American around even though I knew Robert would be devastated to hear about Nigel. Why hadn't I heard from Inspector Reid?

I hung up, turned around, saw the wooden spoon and

rapidly spreading splotches of dark red chili on the floor and headed for the paper towel holder. Then I heard a noise. Somebody was at the door to the service stair, a few feet away from me.

"Who is it?" I asked, telling myself it must be one of the porters picking up the garbage. No answer. This door had no peep hole, so I stood immobilized, listening. I heard a scratching sound at the lock and I called out again. The noise stopped and I let out my breath. Just the porter, checking the door. But why didn't he answer me? There was another brief silence, but I thought I could hear someone breathing on the other side. There was that scratching sound again and a rattle of the knob. I had locked the door, hadn't I? I took a few steps back. Then in one quick movement, the door swung open suddenly and slammed back against the kitchen wall.

Framed in the opening was Nigel.

"How, how, did you get in?" I stammered.

"Child's play," he said with a curled lip. "No porter on the back door, and a simple lock." He slammed the door shut with his foot and started walking toward me.

"What do you want? Why are you here?" I demanded. I was trying to be as brave as possible when all I really wanted to do was scream and run. But where could I run to? He would be right behind me. If I screamed, would anyone hear me? Not with these thick walls.

"You went to the police, didn't you?" he said, standing squarely in front of me.

I wanted to lie, to say no, but he didn't give me a chance.

"I followed you and saw you go in the station," he accused.

"Yes. I just wanted to ask Inspector Reid a few questions, that's all," I said weakly.

"Nosy bitch. Why couldn't you leave it alone? Everything was fine until you put your big American nose into things. Now we're both in trouble."

"Both?"

"They came after me and I've come after you. I got out of the back door of my house while they were still on the doorstep. I'm off to France, but not before I settle up with you for messing up my life. What's one more dead bitch, anyhow?" He was dressed in a dark blazer and slacks—traveling clothes. He had made this detour just to kill me. My mind raced for possibilities to get away. Could I stall him and hope Robert would get here? No, Robert couldn't get here in time. Maybe I could edge past Nigel and run down those back stairs.

He sniffed the air and made a face, then looked toward the stove. "Chili? Bloody swill."

The kitchen telephone's ring startled us both and I started for it, and I lunged for it. So did Nigel, but I grabbed the receiver first, only to have him knock it out of my hand. I cried out in frustration and fear, but he quickly retrieved the dangling receiver and calmly hung it back on its hook. Then he grabbed its cord and gave it a yank, pulling it from the wall.

"Too late to say 'ta ta' now. Or ever!"

I backed away fast, but he moved in closer. "In fact, I think I'll shut your big gawp now and then I'm off to a little place in the Dordogne where they'll never find me."

"You killed Fiona." I needed to keep talking, to stall him, hoping against hope for Robert to make it here. I took a few more steps backward.

"Nobody even suspected that I had been there at her flat until you butted in. The woman actually sacked me from the new S&C account and then laughed at me when I lost my temper. She wanted me to beg. Never! Just a little fall solved the problem. Until you started snooping around with Pauline's list. Now the police want me. But they won't find me. Nigel Newton is not ending up in some dreary cell."

I wanted to get out of that kitchen and closer to the front door because Nigel was planted between me and that back door, and I took a few steps back, but I couldn't edge past the stove without his noticing. I was terrified, heart beginning to pound, blood roaring in my ears. I was trapped.

He stood there with a strange smile on his face. I saw no knife in his hand, but I was frightened that he had brought one of his razor sharp collection, one which could be resting in the pocket of that blazer. Then I remembered that fancy metal strip on the wall, a magnet holding four different size sharp knives. He had only to grab one of them and I was finished. I willed myself not to look at the metal strip that held the set of knives, but my eyes betrayed me. Nigel's eyes followed mine to the rack.

He snorted. "Hah, I wouldn't bother with one of those designer knives. All show. Not sharp enough to do the job I want to do on you. Oh no, I have my own." He patted his blazer pocket.

I desperately tried to take another step away from him, but Nigel suddenly came forward, grabbing both my arms and pushing me back against the stove. I could feel the heat of the pot through my shirt. That hot, heavy pot. It could be a weapon if only I could twist out of his grip. As he took another step closer, his foot clattered against the wooden spoon still lying on the floor and that made him look down. He saw the spoon and the spilled chili, fastidiously pulled his shoe back from the mess and shook his head in disapproval, still looking down.

"Messy cow."

That gave me just enough time to twist away, and with my right hand free I grabbed the handle of the pot and in one quick motion, I whirled and hit him as hard as I could on the side of his face. The heavy pot landed on his nose and cheek, the hot chili splashed in his eyes and he yelled in surprise and pain. He put both hands up to his face, but I hit him again and again on the face and head with that copper pot, even though the metal handle was burning my hand and the hot liquid was splashing all over him and me and the kitchen. He tried to catch my arm, but I was unstoppable. He slumped to the floor, head drooping over his chest, chili mixed with blood running from his nose. I kept hitting him even though he looked knocked out. I was afraid he would reach out and catch my leg, so I made myself put the pot down on the stove and holding my burned hand in the other palm, I ran toward the front door. I had to take off the chain, turn the lock and open the door with that hand, but I did it, sobbing in pain and fright. I ran outside toward the elevator and the stairs. I started screaming then, at the top of my lungs.

A door opposite me opened and a head peered out.

"Call the police, call the police," I yelled. The head retreated.

I kept heading toward the elevator, afraid that Nigel might be right behind me. Had I shut the door as I ran out? Suddenly the elevator at the end of the hall opened and out came Inspector Reid and another man.

"He's there, in the kitchen," I said, pointing. "He tried to kill me! Nigel! I hit him, I hit him with the pot."

Reid and the two men covered the distance quickly and brushed through the half-opened door. I couldn't move, so

I just leaned against the wall. Cowered against the wall. Then Reid came back, put his arm around me and slowly led me to the door of the flat. I pulled back on the threshold, unwilling to face Nigel, but Reid gently urged me into the drawing room. Standing in the middle of the room, face covered in blood and chili, one eye closed, stood Nigel, his hands behind him, swaying slightly in the grip of the policeman holding him. I stared at Nigel, barely able to stand, who looked back at me. There was such hatred in his eyes that I looked away, frightened again.

Suddenly Brack was there, arms around me. "I'm here, Lucy."

I slumped against him, my knees giving away, flinching as Nigel twisted toward me as he was led out of the room. Then my legs did let go, but Brack was still there, arms still holding me tightly as I collapsed against him.

Chapter 24

In the next few hours, Brack fended off the police, telling them I would deal with them tomorrow, got my burned hand treated at the hospital emergency room, brought me back to the flat, gave me some knockout pills and put me to bed. Alone. As I stumbled through all this activity, he told me his story, apparently to keep me moving. He had rung me and heard yelling and then when he tried to call back, the line was dead. He went into action and got through to Reid, just back at the station, and insisted he go to the flat. He got there himself shortly after. I had trouble taking it all in, but thank God they got there before Nigel came after me again. Poor Robert arrived after Nigel had been taken away and Brack put him to work cleaning up the mess. I've lost my appetite for chili. Completely. Will never cook and eat it again. Never.

The next days were full of trips to the police station, statements and more statements, but the excitement finally died down and I got back to work. Inspector Reid and I became quite friendly and he told me that Nigel had called on some of his power friends, got bail and a top lawyer and is fighting the case. He now swears he didn't shove Fiona down the stairs; he says she must have fallen after he had gone out the front door.

Yes, I may have to appear in court and tell what he confessed to me and how he threatened to kill me, but since there were no witnesses to Fiona's tumble, it's his word against mine. I'm being callous again, because I won't mind the experience of testifying in a British court of law—it brings to my mind all those wonderful black-and-white British movies with glamorous stars swathed in furs standing in the witness box. Reid says it won't be like that at all, but I have my dreams. I have also bet him that Nigel will get off or end up with a light sentence. He did try to kill *me* after all and he did have a knife in his blazer pocket. If he's sent to a minimum security prison, he'll probably start cooking gourmet food for the other inmates—all those stockbrokers done for inside trading or company directors who skimmed funds. Then when he gets out he'll get those same people to back him in a new restaurant. Notoriety always helps bring patrons into new restaurants.

The Sweet Whippo campaign finished and it was so successful that I've been offered a full-time job with London Office at a very good salary and an even better title. My family put up a squawk, but I want to try it. Would you believe that before we could start on a follow-up campaign, Sweet Whippo was pulled off the market for "reformulation?" Brack says they are still worried about shelf life.

One of my new assignments is another food account, this one real food, a certain vegetable that the British want to show off to the European Community. It's so secret that I can't talk about it right now.

Brack took me to the Henley Royal Regatta and I looked terrific in a red printed silk dress, the correct length to be allowed into the Stewards' Enclosure, worn with high heels and a spectacular hat. We are back together again; he apologized for his haughty behavior and even admitted I was a good detective, even though I never actually got around to having those chocolates in the freezer analyzed. I just sighed and tossed them out.

"But spare me any more heart-stopping finales like the last one," he begged.

The best thing of all is that Inspector Reid has recommended me for a school for amateur detectives in London, run by an ex-Metropolitan policeman and I've already signed up. My first case is going to be Pauline's suicide. I want to be sure she wasn't done in and I have *my* list of suspects. I might even be able to pin it on Nigel. Remember that chef's jacket in her flat.

Guess who is now going to a wonderful fiction workshop in London, one which specializes in mysteries and suspense? And guess who finally finished that first mystery novel all about food and death and is starting on a second book all about food and death?

About the Author

Elisabeth (Betty) Bastion, a native of Texas, has worked and written for newspapers and magazines in both the U.S. and the United Kingdom. She and her husband, an Englishman, now divide their time between East Hampton, Long Island and England.